Project Found

The Khan Curse: Vol I

Marcus A Broome

ISBN: **0985230312**
ISBN-13: **978-0985230319**

DEDICATION

To Dad

CONTENTS

April 12th, 1990

OUTSKIRTS OF COLUMBUS, OHIO

Crickets' chirps echoed through dense woodland. Heathcliff sat his solid six foot frame against the base of a sycamore tree. Clouds of condensation dissipated after each exhale. With his back to a mile wide field, he chewed on a stick of Juicy Fruit gum and checked his weapons and gear. Behind him, centered in the vast field, stood Heathcliff's objective.

Around him, his team took up their positions along the tree line. Each dressed in black jumpsuits, with matching helmet and an armored vest with the FBI acronym displayed in large bold yellow letters. He turned to face his objective, lifted a pair of binoculars to his eyes with black fingerless gloved hands. He took notice of the large number of guardsmen along the roof and the sixty foot high perimeter fence. A station at each of the four corners carried a high-powered search light. Their lights reached far into the tree line forcing Heathcliff's team to cling to the shadows of the trees. Heathcliff turned his attention to the trees across the field on his far left, the binoculars aimed upwards into the canopy.

He waited a few moments for the signal, but received none. He ducked behind his tree as a beam of light washed over his sector.

The light illuminated his cinnamon skin and the slight fold in the corner of his eyes. His complexion often led people to mistake him for Native American, despite the fact he was of Mongolian and Middle Eastern ancestry. Many under his command jokingly referred to him as Crazy Horse due to his fiery nature in the heat of battle blended with his combat savvy. He took no offense, once hunted his nick-namesake with the US Calvary and took great pride in the comparison.

Encased in darkness again he wiped his nose and glanced back to the tree on his far left. He scanned the canopies again till he saw the signal. A single red light blinked once. He let a minute pass and the light rapidly blinked twice. Heathcliff hid behind the tree as the searchlight returned.

His heart rate picked up and he could feel the adrenaline began to flow. He cherished these tense moments just before battle.

Removing his helmet, he scratched the keloid scar that always itched when perspiration began. The scar was thanks to a Nazi's bullet that cracked his helmet and fractured his skull. He placed the metallic helmet back on his head.

"Everyone, follow me," he called out. "When we move you do not slow down. Full speed till we hit the fence. You all know your assignments. You understand?"

Fifty heads bobbed an affirmative in the night.

Heathcliff stepped out from behind his tree and dashed into the dark open field. The others followed their fearless leader. A wide smile plastered on his face, his legs pumped in tune to the pounding in his chest. Loud pops echoed against the trees and the sound of glass shattering followed and one of the high-powered lights went dark. A searchlight washed over him. His M-16, clutched in his hands, glimmered and another loud pop rang out. The searchlight glass fell from its station and showered the grass below. Bullets rained down on the charging group from the building.

Halfway to his destination a blow took him off his feet and threw his body against the ground gasping for air. Warm liquid seeped from his neck. His mouth filled with the taste of iron and pain shot through his entire body. His eyesight blurred in and out of focus. He concentrated on the stars overhead. Always enjoyed taking his son up to the highest points on earth to gaze at the galaxy. The pain began to subside and he knew this would be his last time to relish in their beauty.

A familiar face blocked his view. His friend's lips moved, but he sounded murky, too far away. Heath opened his mouth to speak. To tell his friend that he would miss him. Instead, blood caught in his throat and he coughed it up. The dire look on his friend's face became more pronounced and he could vaguely make out the shouts surrounding him. The world darkening around him. Another face appeared. She grabbed his hand and squeezed. He could not muster up the strength to squeeze back. A third person joined them; he immediately pulled bandages out of his pack.

Heathcliff smiled as the faces faded into the night sky. On this battlefield stuck in an eternal struggle between good and evil, he could not envision a better way to die.

Wyndell listened to the words coming over the radio. His father, the man he fought beside for decades was now dead, words he foolishly felt he would never hear. The man was a winner and had survived more close calls than he could count. A shorter darker version of his old man, thanks to his petite Black mother's genes, Wyndell always pictured himself the same way. Invincible.

"He's dead. You're in charge now," the voice repeated in his ear. "Your orders, sir!"

Wyndell snapped out of his trance. He stared at the enemy below him. His group orders were to wait till his father's unit hit the fence. The enemy below didn't even notice them. Someone's failure to remind their grounded allies to always check the heavens. His thick lips quivered and his blood boiled with vengeance.

"We move on with the mission," he whispered into the radio.

He jammed the butt of his M-16 into his shoulder and clicked the safety off. He signaled for those around him to do the same. He tried to control his shaking body, but his rage quickly consumed him. With a throaty roar, he pulled the trigger and charged his enemy.

Dirk Payce's rigid six foot two frame shifted anxiously from side to side in front of his station, a light blue door. Behind the door were four little reasons this laboratory existed. Now that existence had come to an abrupt end and he had front row seats.

A symphony of utter chaos swelled around him. Heels clicked, shoes shuffled and boots stomped against the tiled floor. The popping of computers' hard drives exploding and sporadic gunfire blended with the crackling fire. Screams and angry shouts responded in rhythm to every pop and boom that shook the building. Smoke clung to the ceiling.

Over the radio, voices battled with each other to convey information to one another. From what he could pick out the south side had been breached along with the rooftop. The voices on the rooftop sounded as surprised as he that they got people on the roof so quickly. He heard no mention of a helo let alone heard one himself.

However, it wasn't the chaos that had him anxious. Years in the Special Forces prepared him for chaos. No, it was the job he had the unfortunate honor to have thrust upon him. He looked for confirmation before he made the unpopular move.

Down the hall amongst the fleeing scientists, Dirk noticed the scientist in charge. He was clearly being chastised by some old frail man in a wheelchair. Behind the wheelchair bound man stood a much younger man, mirroring the disappointment on the old man's face. The scientist, Dr. Nathaniel Porter, looked as disheveled as you expect a man whose dreams were literally burning around him to look. The man in the wheelchair and his companion turned away from Dr. Porter and disappeared into the crowd. Porter forced his way through the crowd.

Dirk stepped into the doctor's path to get his attention. The doctor stopped, his face red and his mouth twisted in a snarl.

"What?" He barked into the hired gun's face.

"The subjects. Am I to terminate?" He feared the answer to come.

"Fifteen fucking years," Porter shouted to no one. "Done in less than an hour!"

"Sir."

Porter jabbed a finger into the mercenary's chest.

"You do your job. Leave nothing behind," he walked away.

Dirk reluctantly nodded and watched the defeated doctor become engulfed by the panic stricken crowd. Dirk faced the door he's been guarding. He reached out and twisted the doorknob. The soft cries of children washed over him.

The door shut behind him and he walked into the center of the room. There were four twin size beds, two against each wall on his right and left, each bed adorned in cartoon sheets. Huddled together, on the bed in the far right corner, were four weeping children. Dirk unclasp the holster on his hip and pulled out his stainless steel Colt Double Eagle pistol. His hand shook as the gun rose up and the weapon's sights trained in on the innocent huddle.

"No!" One of the tiny four year olds cried out while the others whined.

Dirk had killed many men, even some brazen women, but never a child. Staring down the barrel he wondered how to choose. His mind wrestled with the dilemma. Vision blurred, he blinked the tears away. He let out a frustrated shout and dropped his hands. The kids exhaled cautiously.

"Who the hell orders someone to kill a child?" Dirk shouted. He rushed over to one of the vacant beds and flipped it over on its side. "Fucker should handle it himself. You want them dead? You do it!" He shouted to the door.

Holstering his gun he turned to face the kids.

"Come on," he waved his empty hand towards the door. The kids hesitated. "I'm getting you out of here. Come on!"

The four jumped off the bed and ran to him. He scooped them up in his massive arms and opened the door to an empty smoke filled hallway. Outside the gunfire continued unabated. He took them past a few burning rooms to a door on the north end where, according to radio communications, action was light. The solid metal door creaked open and he stuck his head out to survey their surroundings. The grounds appeared calm compared to the firefight on the other side. He opened the door wider and let the kids out. Dirk took a couple steps forward. His head exploded, stunning the little ones just ahead of him. Blood, skull, and brain matter smacked against the metal door with a wet thud. His body crumpled before them. They screamed and ran off into the darkness.

April 14th, 1990

COLUMBUS, OHIO

Jamila cupped the wine glass between her hands. In the midst of another long night full of infomercials and phone sex line ads, she shifted in her recliner sofa chair to alleviate the pain along her midsection. There was little for her to do, however, to quell the sorrow in her heart.

She glanced at the orange container, beside her bottle of wine, filled with prescription painkillers. The label, warning against alcohol consumption, stared back at her.

"To hell with labels and vows," she thought to herself and took a sip. *"He said till death,"* she drunk from the glass again. *"I'm still breathing."*

She was referring to her ex-husband. He left her a couple weeks before her surgery. The doctor's grim revelation that due to her age, thirty-five, and the surgery; their chances of a successful pregnancy was non-existence. Well, he couldn't abide that and left to find himself a 'younger, healthier' woman.

Her eyes locked with the bottle again. She remember her final thought just before her surgery. That maybe the anesthesiologist got the dosage wrong and she would not wake to face this new, empty life.

A knock at the door jolted Jamila from her dark thoughts. She placed her glass down beside the pill bottle. "What the hell?" She slurred her words.

A quick glance at her watch informed her of the odd hour for visitors. She kicked off her afghan blanket as another series of raps shook her front door. Jamila climbed out her recliner and groaned in pain. Her arms rubbed the bandage along her midsection.

She grabbed her robe off the back of the chair and stepped into her slippers. Tightening the robe around her flannel pajamas she steady herself against the sudden swirl in her mind. Another set of knocks struck her door.

"I'm coming!" She shouted at the door.

Shuffling along the hardwood floor she reached the door. Peering through the peephole, a man in a pea coat and suit stood between two uniformed officers. She opened the door till the door's chain caught.

"What do you want?" She asked.

"Mrs. Foster?" The suit asked.

"I go by Ms. Dunne now," She corrected.

"My apologies for the inconvenience, Ms. Dunne," he reached into his pocket and retrieved his credentials. "I'm Special Agent Wyndell Caan, of the BCI," he turned to the officer on his right. "Turner, you can bring everything up."

Both officers nodded and moved off the porch to their squad car parked in front. Jamila studied the wide shouldered agent. Her job as a social worker had her cross path with the Bureau of Criminal Investigation, but never outside of the workplace.

"May I come in Ms. Dunne?" He asked.

Jamila dropped her eyes. Realized he caught her staring at him. *"Of course when I'm trying to drown my pain, police show up at my door."* She shut the door and released the chain. Using the door for support she opened it slowly.

Wyndell stepped through door. Jamila shut the door behind him and led him out of the foyer into her living room. She stood beside her recliner while he surveyed her home. He clasped his hands behind his back.

"Lovely home you have," he commented.

"It's not much of a home anymore," she countered.

"That feeling will be temporary."

Her front door opened and she heard the sound of light footsteps against her hardwood floor. Four small children appeared from her foyer. They each wore sunglasses and blue jumpers. They stopped once they reached Wyndell and stood beside him.

"What is this?" She asked.

The officers appeared after the kids. They carried duffel bags and placed them beside the kids and Wyndell. One of them handed Wyndell a briefcase.

"Thank you," he said and accepted the briefcase. "That'll be all. You two can go. I told my partner to pick me up here." The officers looked to one another and shrugged.

"You're welcome," Turner said. "Need anything else we won't be far."

"What is going on?" Jamila asked after the officers exited her home.

"You should probably take a seat," Wyndell suggested.

"Why should I? And why did you bring four little kids into my home?" She could not tear her eyes away from the four children. The sunglasses at night bothered her.

"Because, they are yours," he informed her.

Jamila shut her eyes as the words sunk in. She felt her body sway and placed a hand on her recliner. "I've had a lot to drink before you showed up," she explained opening her eyes. "Did you say they are mines? I don't have any kids."

"Ms. Dunne, please have a seat."

Jamila turned around and walked into her kitchen. Wyndell followed her, the kids followed him. She pulled a chair out for him. A small jolt of pain reminded her to move gingerly.

"How is the healing process going?" He asked.

"How do you know?" Jamila took a seat across the table from Wyndell.

"There's not much I don't know, Ms. Dunne."

Her eyes shifted back to the children. They sat on her tiled floor against the refrigerator. They huddled together resting their heads on each other.

"Why are you here Agent Caan?"

"To give you the family you'd lost, twice."

"Give me what?" Jamila asked.

Wyndell placed the briefcase on the table. He reached across the table and took the woman's hand in his. She felt the warmth of his hand warm hers.

"That watch on your wrist," he lifted her hand.

The hand dial watch, with its worn leather strap, ticked as she stared at it.

"Your father gave that to you a month before he died," he ran his thumb along her knuckles.

She could feel an energy run through her. She gripped his fingers and her heart pounded in her chest. The beep of the machine that kept her father alive as he handed her the watch echoed. "I can hear the machine," her voice cracked.

"That was the end of your first family. Your mother died when you were only six."

Jamila held her breath as the beeping in her ears turned into a beautiful song. A song she has not heard for almost thirty years. She could feel the warmth of her mother's arm around her. Her ear tingled in response to her mother's warm breath.

"Despite your extended families' reluctance to accept you, because of the mixing of Arab and Irish blood, you persevered. It's why you chose the career you're in. Help those with no family, have what you could not."

He released her hand and Jamila felt the heat leave her body. She took deep breaths, her whole body shivered, and she tightened her robe around her. Her face wet with tears she did not know she shed. She wiped at her face with her sleeves.

"Oh my god!" She exclaimed. "What did you do to me? What was that?"

"Jamila, after your surgery which has left you incapable of having children. I am giving you a third chance."

She looked at the four children. She assumed they were asleep. Their chest rose and fell slowly. "Why me?" She asked.

"Throughout your life you've battle hardship, but your good nature never faltered. I sense unrivaled strength in you. I know you will be exactly what they need. You will keep them safe."

"Safe?"

"These kids are special."

"How?"

"We found them along the Alum Creek exit ramp on highway two seventy. There was a raid not too far from there. There are things about these kids I can't explain."

"I find that hard to believe after what you just did to me," Jamila looked over at the kids again. "What's with the sunglasses?"

"I need you to focus," Wyndell grabbed the briefcase and unlocked it. He lifted it open and pulled out four folders. "We drafted up identities for them."

Jamila took the folders. "What do you want from me?"

"Leave the city."

"What? I can't just get up and leave. I have a career here and I just had surgery. I don't have the money to..."

Wyndell spun the open briefcase to face Jamila. She fell silent at the sight of hundred dollar bills stacked inside the briefcase.

"How much is that?" She asked.

"In here, roughly five hundred thousand," he answered. "There's more in the duffel bags. Altogether you have one point eight million dollars."

"Million?"

"More than enough to begin a new life," Wyndell stood up from the table. "There's one rule, if you must take them to a doctor. Find one you can trust. Or use the money to buy his trust, if you have to."

Wyndell headed back into the living room towards the foyer. Jamila got out of her chair and followed him. "Wait a minute, that's it? You're leaving me with four kids to raise on my own?"

"You'll be fine," he called back over his shoulder and turned into the foyer.

"What if I need your help? Do I call the BCI?"

Wyndell stopped at the door and looked back at Jamila. "I think we both know by now I am not with the BCI."

"Then how do I get in contact with you?"

"Ms. Dunne, it was nice meeting you. This is your family, congratulations."

Wyndell opened the door and stepped outside.

"You can't just give me a shit ton of money and kids and just leave!" Jamila rushed to the door as it shut. She opened it and stepped out onto the porch.

She stood alone. No sign of Special Agent Wyndell Caan. She stepped off the porch and stood in her front yard. The street was bare. She heard soft footsteps behind her and turned around.

The four children stared at her, basked in the light of her porch light. She walked back to the porch and sat on the steps. One of the two girls walked up to Jamila. She stood out from the group. She was all white. From her hair to her porcelain skin. The other three were varying shades of brown.

"What is with the sunglasses?" She asked the little girl.

"He said, it was to keep from scaring the cops."

Jamila sucked her teeth and took the girl's sunglasses off. "Oh... wow," she said.

September 20th 2002

EVANSVILLE, OHIO
SEVENTY-FIVE MILES WEST OF COLUMBUS
6:23AM

Jamila Dunne stared out the window above her kitchen sink at her manicured backyard. A single tree in the yard swayed in the last of the summer winds. Water from the faucet poured over soapy dishes clearing away the morning's syrupy breakfast.

Upstairs were her four little blessings. She could hear them giggling and stomping about. Unlike most teenagers around this time of year, they were excited to head back to school. After a couple years of homeschooling and tutors, they were anxious to get out of the house and be able to enjoy their senior year with their classmates.

She looked at her watch, shut the faucet off, and made her way to the staircase. "Hurry up you four," she called out softly.

She learned early on not to bother raising her voice. Her four children had exceptional hearing.

Feet stomped, giggles abounded and the four teens appeared at the top of the stairs.

"Move, Mom," Tundra shouted, franticly waving her arms. "I have to show you this."

Jamila stepped back. She was not sure what the girl had in mind, but the four never ceased to amaze her. Tundra leapt from the top of the stairs. Jamila's heart stopped and she gasped. Tundra's long black hair spread out like a sail caught in the wind. She stuck her landing at the bottom of the staircase and Jamila let out a breath of relief.

"Yeah," Tundra turned around to gloat in front of her siblings. "No stairs! Now what?"

Jamila moved in front of Tundra and glared at the others. She could see the anxiousness in their eyes to match Tundra's feat. Jamila put her hand up.

"No one else better try that!" She yelled. She grabbed Tundra's arm and locked in to her daughter's hazel eyes. "Don't you ever do that again. You nearly scared me to death."

"Sorry," Tundra dropped her eyes; her voice a soft whisper.

"The rest of you come down the stairs like you got some sense."

They walked down the steps and went to retrieve their backpacks. They did not resemble each other, the only exception being Timber and Mackenzie, both boys clearly of African descent. They could have been brothers. However, Tundra appeared to be Hispanic. Caspian, who went by Cassie and sometimes Snow, due to her creamy white complexion and white hair; displayed heterochromia. One eye blue and the other green, a trait the others did not exhibit.

6:35AM

Jamila opened the front door and the four teens blew past her onto the stone walkway. Backpacks hung off of one shoulder, and they chattered happily amongst themselves. She locked the door and followed them to the station wagon waiting in the driveway.

"Shotgun!" Tundra called out.

"Mom?!" Cassie whined. Her waist length white hair flowed around her blue 'South Park' Professor Chaos tee.

"She called it, Snow," Jamila stomped out the complaint as quickly as it arose.

Cassie groaned her displeasure, but obeyed and headed to the rear doors with her brothers. Tundra stopped with her hand on the passenger door and noticed a service van parked two houses down. The company logo painted on the side of the van read 'Tony's Air Duct Cleaners'.

"How long does it take for someone to get their ducts cleaned?" She asked while waiting for her mother unlock the doors.

Jamila popped opened the locks with a press of the keyless entry pad. She looked over at the van and shrugged her shoulders. She opened her door and got inside.

"I don't know, maybe a couple hours," she said once everyone were inside.

"Well, that truck has been in front of the Peters house for a couple days," Tundra remarked and secured her seat belt with a click.

"Everybody buckled up?" Jamila asked.

The kids gave her a collective affirmative and she turned the car's engine on. The ninety-eight blue Subaru Legacy roared to life and she backed out onto the residential road. She drove past the service van and noticed Tundra's interest in it.

"Maybe they just have a really dirty house," she assured her.

"I guess," the unconvinced girl fiddled with one of the straps of her orange backpack in her lap.

To distract herself, she reached into the glove compartment and pulled out a black CD wallet. She flipped through and found the CD she was looking for. She loaded it into the car's audio system and soon Coldplay's In My Place purred through the speakers. Tundra and her siblings softly bobbed their heads to the beat.

Jamila checked the kids out of the corner of her eyes. They were quietly enjoying their music and she began to question if she should go over her speech once more. She felt she made her points clear last night, but she was not sure if her words truly sunk in to them. The music clicked off and she noticed Tundra staring at her.

"Out with it," Tundra said.

"Can't enjoy the music with you being all antsy over there," Mackenzie pointed out. His impressively low voice rumbled in the car.

"Okay," Jamila always found their ability to read her unnerving. "Well, I just want to reiterate what I said last night."

The kids groaned loudly.

"I knew it was the 'be good' speech," Mac complained. "I should have put money on that."

"Well it is. I had to beg the school board to let you four back into the school system. I don't know what happened with you four, but the past three years you guys have raised hell."

"Hell sounds like such a harsh word," Cassie interjected.

"How else should I describe two years of expulsion, probation for property damage and assault?" The car remained silent.

"I need you four to be like you were before your hormones sent you into permanent hulk mode," she pleaded. "You could've graduated from high school last year if it wasn't for your eagerness to accept every challenge lain at your feet. Do you know how special it is to graduate at fourteen? You could be in any ivy league school of your choice right now."

"I get it Mom, we're fuck ups," Timber muttered, with the collar of his blue Cleveland Indians T-shirt in his mouth.

"What? No Timber," the hyperbolic boy always took things the hardest out of the group. "I just want this year to go smoothly. I want to be able to watch you guys walk across the stage."

The high school appeared on the horizon. Cassie pulled the collar out of Timbers mouth. He nodded, knowing his nervous habit annoyed her.

Jamila hands squeezed the steering wheel.

"We'll make it," Tundra assured her. She watched Jamila's hands loosen on the steering wheel.

"We don't want to fight. But we won't stand for anyone bullying us," Cassie pointed out.

"Next time, instead of handling it yourselves, try telling a teacher."

She steered the car into the school's parking lot and stopped at the main entrance. All around them large yellow school buses were unloading kids.

Jamila turned to Tundra with open arms.

"Come on, give me a hug and a kiss," she gestured for Tundra to come to her.

Tundra unbuckled herself and leaned over to embrace her mother. They exchange a quick peck on their cheeks before releasing one another. Jamila turned to face the others in the backseat. She stuck her arm out and three hands clasped hers.

"Be good."

"We will," Mac said and opened his car door.

Jamila reached and touched Timber's face. They locked eyes for a moment and she gave him a smile.

"You are not a fuck up."

Timber returned the smile and nodded. He followed his brother and sisters out of the car. The blue Subaru pulled away from the curb as they waved farewell.

7:05AM

"Oh snap! The rumor mill was telling the truth," Terrance Pilts, a fourteen year old kid with blond hair, green eyes and a light brown summer tan, called out.

The Dunne kids turned around to see Terrance make his way towards them. Neither recognized him at first. The last time they saw him he was around their height. The boy before them stood at a wiry six feet.

"Terrance?" Mackenzie asked.

"Fuck yeah! Mac, how are you doing?" They locked hands in a quick handshake.

"I'm good."

"You are tall!" Cassie blushed at her hurried words and tried not to stare at the boy's physique.

"Yeah, I hit a growth spurt during the spring," he observed his schoolmates. "You guys did not."

"Fuck you," Mac said and shoved his friend.

"Man I haven't seen you four since ya'll went into hiding after beating that gang down over the summer. Did you end up in jail or something?"

"Jail?" Tundra shook her head. Her black hair draped over her tight red American Eagle shirt.

"Naw," Mac answered. "A gang going to the cops? Not happening."

"Well everybody has been talking about you guys. You got people scared you're going to beat the whole school up."

"We didn't fight that much," Cassie sounded mortified. "Did we?"

"I'm starting to think we have a problem," Timber commented.

"A problem? Naw, you guys are awesome," Terrance countered. "You are like the Jason Bourne of Evansville. Did you see that movie? It was so cool."

"We have to go see the principal, Terrance," Tundra pointed to the large bricked building behind the skinny boy.

"In trouble already?" He joked.

"Shut up," Tundra playfully shoved the boy and walked past him, unaware that she nearly knocked him over.

7:13AM

They sat in four chairs set up in front of the Principal's desk. Impatiently they waited for Principal Stines to show up. Eyes shifted over the pictures and degrees that adorned the yellow wallpaper. The office appeared different from their last visit almost three years ago. Tundra stood up from her seat and grabbed one of the many framed photos on the man's desk.

"Whoa, look at that," she showed her siblings the photo in her hands.

"Little Tosha is getting big."

"What is she now, twelve?" Cassie took the photo from her sister for a closer look.

Footsteps alerted them to Stines impending appearance and Cassie swiftly returned the photo back to its original position. The door opened and Stine stared at the young fresh faces looking back at him.

"Stines, my man," Mac said with a confident grin. His eyes followed the principal to his chair behind the desk. "Long time no see."

"That's Principal Stines to you," Derrick Stines, a short rotund middle aged white male with thinning brown hair, corrected him.

"I'm guessing this isn't going to be quick," Tundra frowned.

"I want to stress to you four just how short your leash is."

All four slouched in their seats.

"We get it, we have to be on our best behaviors," Mac whined. "Two strikes, I know baseball."

"Two strikes is correct," Stines opened a drawer and pulled out four folders held together by rubber bands. The folders hit the desk with a loud thud. "This is the record you have built up in this building since you've entered it."

"I guess we do have a problem," Cassie said, looking to Timber who stared back at her with his collar clenched between his teeth.

"That's an understatement," Stines opened the folder and picked up a sheet of paper. "Timber Dunne, cost the school thousands when he decided to dunk and bring down the backboard."

Timber pulled his shirt from his mouth and sat up.

"I can see you are still angry about that..." he began.

"That was two years ago," Mac interrupted.

Timber slapped his brother's thigh.

"I agree that what I did was wrong and I will never do it again. However, let's all agree that was one spectacular dunk. I mean I was only five three when I did that. Don't let the growth spurt fool you."

"Growth spurt?" Cassie asked. "You grew three inches. Terrance, now he had a growth spurt."

"So did I," Timber emphasized.

Cassie crossed her arms.

"Still short," she countered.

Mac leaned forward in his seat. "The man said he had a growth spurt. Let him have this."

Tundra chuckled. "Wow," she feigned whispering in Cassie's ear. "Tiny sticking up for small over here."

"Whoa, I am taller than him," Mac stated.

"Like hell you are," Timber snapped.

Mac glared at his brother.

"You want to do this?" He challenged.

Timber stepped on the heel of his sneaker with the other and pulled a foot free.

"Shoes off let's go," he accepted.

"Enough!" Stines shouted. Timber slipped his foot back into his shoe. "Timber I want you to control yourself. If any of you step out of line in any fashion, you will be done in the Evansville school district."

"It won't happen," Tundra assured him. "Can we get our schedules? I don't want us to be late on our first day back."

Stines pulled the schedules from his pocket and handed them over.

"I don't want to see you four in here ever again."

The kids nodded and agreed on their way out the office.

10:13AM

Cassie quietly made her way down the hallway bordered by green lockers. She walked shoulder to shoulder with her fellow classmates, their irrelevant conversations humming in her ears.

Her first couple of classes went by without an incident. Pleased with herself she envisioned a brilliant senior year. She fantasized about Terry asking her to the prom and then shook the idea out of her head. She looked around to see if anyone noticed, then chuckled at the foolish thought that anyone could read her mind.

"Cassie," a voice called out behind her and startled the white haired girl.

Cassie turned to see Coach Brentley making her way through the crowd. The middle aged woman coached females' soccer, field hockey, and basketball teams in the school along with teaching gym. She stood just a couple inches taller than Cassie, but her strong physique and fierce eyes made sure no one questioned her orders. Her brown hair bobbed on her shoulders with each step. Even the way she walked appeared like an exercise.

"Where's your sister?" Brentley asked once in front of Cassie.

Coach chewed powerfully on a stick of gum. Cassie stared at the muscles in the woman's jaw clench and release. She couldn't tell if Brentley was enjoying the gum or trying to give her already square jaw more definition.

"On her way to AP Calculus," she pointed in the direction from which Brentley just came. "Speaking of which I have to make it to Chemistry before the bell rings. You know I'm on a short leash, Coach."

"Don't worry about it; I'll write you a note. Look, I'm going to get to the chase. I want you and your sister to play for us."

"In what?"

"Everything! We were so close to state for the first time ever in your freshman year. Then you know..."

Cassie just nodded. She didn't want the memory of their expulsion clouding a good day.

"You two let your teammates down. Many of them are gone now without experiencing a championship, but these girls, you can help give them that moment. They're not going to get it without you two."

"Even field hockey?"

"No, unfortunately none of the parents are comfortable with you two in contact sports with their little girls."

Cassie rolled her eyes.

"Hey, I agree with them young lady. I've seen the way you two were out there. You're like rabid dogs. I swear you two could break me in half if you wanted too."

"No, way Coach. You got first place in that Miss Body competition once."

The bell rang.

"Twice. So do you think you two can help us out this year? I think you can bring home a lot of trophies to this school," Coach Brentley took out a pad and pen and began writing.

Cassie smiled at the thought. She enjoyed playing sports. She knew Coach's words were true. They never tasted defeat. She and Tundra dominated the field of play with such ease that their opponents' wills were often crushed in the opening minutes of any game. To win a couple championships, go to prom with Terrance... or anyone, and graduate with honors would make her year.

"Yeah! Definitely, we would love to play this year. Just have to check with my mom and if she gives the go ahead. Yes."

"Good," Brentley ripped the paper out of the pocket sized pad and handed it to Cassie. "Once you get the go ahead from your mom you and your sister come to my office. We'll get you set up for soccer."

11:45AM

Mac scribbled idly in his notebook. He tried anything to keep his head focused on one thing. The teacher went on about the universe and many scientists' theories on its existence and, inevitably, ours. Mac already checked out the moment he noticed his dream's sweet fragrance of apples and cinnamon. She sat just in front of him one row to his left. Any normal classroom he would be able to stare at the back of her head without a care. This teacher, Ms. Eppic, divided her room in half. Four rows, three chairs to a row, against parallel walls facing the center of the room.

Mac felt it was some cruel trick the teacher plotted to test his discipline. For the first forty minutes of class his eyes drifted to her several times. A couple times she almost caught him. He decided to keep his eyes on his notebook.

His will melting, his eyes lifted back to her. He soaked in her beauty once more. Long light brown hair that reached the middle of her back. Her skin, baked by the summer sun, glowed a dark brown. Her radiant green eyes followed the teacher up and down the center aisle of the room. Mac's eyes jumped to follow the teacher as she walked past. His hand moved the pen along the notebook's paper. His mind drifted back to the first time he smelled the girl's sweet fragrance.

Two months ago

Timber dribbled the ball up court. They were down to the last possession in their daily marathon full court pick-up games. Mac wiped sweat from his eyes and jogged over to cover his brother. They jostled for position at the half court line.

Timber performed a swift crossover that would've 'broken' the ankle of any normal kid, but Mac quickly recovered. He sidestepped till he was in front of his brother again. A strong stiff arm jolted Timber back to the half court line. He lost his dribble and took his number of allotted steps.

"Fuck!" Timber exclaimed at his predicament, confined to his pivot foot on the line.

Mac laughed and moved in to apply pressure. Tundra called out for the ball with Cassie smothering her. Timber lifted the ball to pass it, but Mac kept his hands between them.

"Come on, take a step," Mac taunted, pushing his chest into his brother's, forcing him off balance.

"Fuck this," Timber put his arm between them and leaned into Mac.

The two struggled against each other for a few moments. Timber forced his sweaty head against Mac's shoulder, creating separation. He lifted his elbow and drove it into Mac's ribs. The blow lifted Mac up and out of Timber's face. With a clear shot of the basket Timber jumped with Mac draped all over him.

"I believe!" Timber shouted and released the ball at the peak of his jump.

All four, and the small crowd that gathered to witness their legendary pick-up games, watched the ball sail at a high arc towards the basket. With a soft swish the leather ball fell through the hoop hitting nothing but nylon net.

Mac shoved his brother away from him. The crowd and Tundra rushed Timber to congratulate him on the shot. Mac bent over to catch his breath. They always played to a hundred and it normally took them three to four hours to complete a game. He enjoyed the constant movement and muscle spasms afterwards.

"No," a voice shouted in the distance. "Don't you fucking put your hands on me."

Mac tracked the voice and noticed a girl surrounded by a group of men a couple courts down. He stepped towards her. Cassie called out to him, but he continued to make his way towards the damsel.

"Mac," Cassie grabbed her brother's shoulder. "I know you're not mad, are you?"

"No," Mac never slowed his stride. "She's in trouble."

Cassie looked beyond her brother and noticed what caught his attention. She spun around and called to Tundra and Timber, then jogged to catch up with her brother.

"Look," the girl stood her ground. "You are not going to intimidate me. My brother is coming home with me."

"Jessica, just leave, alright?" Her younger brother, a tall lanky light brown kid with a reddish afro, demanded.

"I'm not leaving without you. Mama said she don't want you out here with them."

"Look bitch, the man made up his mind," Pipe, the infamous high school dropout and drug dealer as well as addict, pressed himself against Jessica.

She pushed the smelly white boy off of her. She took a step back and bumped into a fat man in baggy jeans and a Reds baseball cap. He reached out to grab her ass. Jessica slapped his hand away.

"Marvin," she called out to her brother, who just slunk away.

"Yo," Mac called out. His voice boomed over the now hyped up group.

Mac's siblings quickly lined up on each side of him. They could sense that the energy had picked up and the gang was bound to release it.

"Oh shit," Pipe exclaimed and chuckled at the sight. "Mighty mice to the fucking rescue!"

The gang laughed at their leader's joke.

"What are you little fuckers going to do? This is grown folks business."

"You know something?" Mac stepped up to Pipe. His lips curled in disgust. "I hate being called little."

"Mackenzie Dunne, do you find something fascinating up there?" Ms. Eppic asked the daydreaming boy.

Mac snapped out of his daze at the sudden sound of his name. He realized he been staring at the ceiling. Around him his classmates laughed.

"Sorry," Mac apologized.

The teacher went back to her lecture when suddenly the bell rang. All the students stood up to leave. The quiet room exploded into lively conversations. Kids poured out of the room. Mac stuffed his books into this backpack and stood up. He headed towards the door and stopped in front of her desk.

She had her backpack on her shoulders and was chatting away with one of her friends. She didn't noticed Mac until she walked right into him.

"Sorry," Mac quickly spat out.

"No I'm sorry," she said and brushed her hair behind her ear. She smiled and locked eyes with the young man. "I should have been watching where I was going."

"No, you're fine," Mac insisted. "I just wanted to know how everything turned out with your brother."

"Everything's fine."

"They haven't messed with ya'll or anything?" He stepped back to allow her by.

"No, after that beating you gave them I don't think they'll be back," she stepped by him and headed for the door.

Mac stepped in sync with her. "That was nothing, barely had to try. I'm sure they were more scared of having to go up against you again."

"I seriously doubt that."

"Naw, I'm for real, you got some serious ovaries on you girl."

"Excuse me, what?" Jessica stopped and her face scrunched up in disgust.

Mac flinched and shook his head. "No, I was just saying. Like juevos, you know balls."

"What?"

"Not that you have balls, per say," Mac looked up to the ceiling and cleared his throat.

"Because I don't."

"I know, that's why I said ovaries. Because women sexual organs are..."

"Why are you talking about my sexual organs?" Jessica shifted her feet and placed a hand on her hip.

Mac sighed and brought his gaze back to Jessica's green eyes.

"I don't know. I just came here to ask you to a movie. Like the Bourne Identity or something."

Jessica smiled and shook her head. "I'm sorry. I already have a boyfriend and you are too young for me."

Mac tried to hide the pain with a smile. "Sure," he said.

Mac watched her walk away. He apologized as she went by without a word. She met with her friend at the door who asked what had happened. Mac looked over his shoulder to see the teacher staring at his failure. The teacher tried to hide it by focusing on the papers on top of her projector.

Mac dipped his head and walked out of the classroom.

12:04PM

Timber lifted his head up to catch the menagerie of smells emanating from the kitchen. He stood in the middle of a long line of chattering teenagers. His stomach growled anxiously awaiting his turn.

Smells of baked blueberry crumble, mashed potatoes, peas, butter and a slab of generic meat covered in lumpy gravy swirled around him. The sign outside the kitchen read 'Salisbury Steak', but his nostrils told him otherwise. Despite the low grade in food quality, he still found himself eager to consume all of it.

Mac stepped into line behind his brother to the chagrin of the students behind them. He leaned against the cream colored cinderblock wall.

Timber looked over his shoulder and read his brother's expression.

"What you moping about?" He asked and shuffled forward with the line.

"Nothing," Mac crossed his arms and moved along with his brother.

"Oh it's something to have you pouting like a girl," Timber noticed

Mac's cheek twitch at the last word.

"Ha. It's a girl!"

Mac pushed his brother forward. "Shut up Timberland!"

"Don't tell me," Timber stared at his brother's face. "Who shut you down? Is it the girl you haven't shut up about? It has to be."

Mac reluctantly nodded his head. Timber raised his arms in victory. Mac delivered a quick jab to his brother's open rib cage. Timber groaned in pain and cradled his torso in his arms.

"Don't take pleasure in my pain," Mackenzie muttered.

"Not cool," Timber groaned, rubbing the sore spot.

"Besides, she didn't really shut me down," he reasoned with himself.

Timber gave a sympathetic nod.

"She got a boyfriend. So not like she had a choice. I'll get her. You'll..."

Cassie's and Tundra's laughter alerted both boys. The girls made their way down the line and joined their brothers, oblivious to those waiting in line. The girls' glee annoyed Mac and they quickly noticed.

"What is with you?" Tundra asked.

"Oh, he's just experiencing a little achy breaky heart," Timber teased.

"Learn to shut your mouth," Mac warned. "What got you two so happy?"

"We are going to bring the state championship home!" Cassie cheered.

"As many as they allow. We're going to stack the shelves."

"Why don't you two join a sport, and help us fill this place with gold before we go?" Tundra wondered.

"You know how they always gotta penalize us for being too good," Mac reminded her. "That homecoming game was epic."

"Yeah, remember how the parents complained after that homecoming game?" Timber stepped back. "Mom pulled Mac and me out, because we were making the papers too much."

"Well, don't hit so hard then," Cassie suggested.

"Timber, I think you got pit stains," Tundra pointed at his armpits.

"What?" Timber lifted his arms to check for stains.

Tundra took off her backpack and slipped it onto Timber's arm.

"No," she answered. "But you can find us a place to sit and eat before all the chairs are taken."

Mac and Cassie quickly dumped their packs on Timber. He opened his mouth to complain, but thought better of it and accepted he was fooled.

"Go on," Mac urged with a pleased grin.

Timber rolled his eyes and began walking towards the cafeteria. "Don't fuck this up!" Tundra called out.

They laughed watching their brother disappear into the crowded lunchroom. Someone tapped Cassie's shoulder and she turned to see Terrence standing in front of her. Their eyes met and lingered. Blood rushed to her face, she laughed harder and turned away from him.

"Terry, get your ass in line!" Mac shouted and pulled his friend into the line with them. "You got lunch this period too?"

"Yeah," Terry said. His eyes scanned the impatient glares from their classmates behind them.

"What is with you?" Tundra whispered to Cassie.

"Nothing," Cassie giggled, her pale skin turning a rosy red.

"No, not Terry," Tundra said with wide eyes.

"What the fuck are you two going on about?" Mac asked.

"Got our seats marked," Timber announced.

"Professor Chaos?" Terry pointed to Cassie's shirt. "I love that guy."

Cassie nodded, tried to shrink the wide grin on her face. "Me too.

Butters, he's a riot," She giggled.

"A riot?" Timber's forehead wrinkled. "Who fucking says that?"

"Shut up, Timber," Cassie shoved her brother.

The group stood outside the kitchen doors and Timber slipped to the front of the group. His stomach growled again. Once inside the kitchen he grabbed a Styrofoam tray and instructed the servers to dump everything on it. At the end of the servers' line he grabbed a bottle of Fruitopia and paid for his meal.

He emerged from the kitchen into the cafeteria. The room rumbled with the roar of rambunctious teenagers. A handful of teachers peppered the room to keep a semblance of order. The rich smell of blueberry crumble on his plate beckoned him and he jammed a finger into the warm goo.

His siblings and Terry joined him in the cafeteria.

"Where to, Timber?" Tundra asked.

Timber finished sucking the goo from his finger and nodded toward the far end of the room. "All the way in the back. Away from everyone, so no one can mess with us," he explained.

Tundra took the lead and the four followed. Timber continued to dip into his blueberry crumble. They pushed their way through the crowded lunchroom. Kids laughed and yelled to one another. At one table a group of kids were busy freestyling, while another drummed out a beat on the table with a pen and his fist.

Tundra stopped once they reached the last table in the cafeteria. Seated at the table were five large boys with matching jackets on. They boasted and stuffed their mouths with all the food they could fit.

"Timber?" Tundra mumbled.

Timber took his finger out of his mouth. Most of his blueberry delight was gone.

"Whoa," he moved up beside her. "Before you go getting all pissed, the seats were empty and I put our bags on the chairs. The fuckers must've moved them."

"Assholes!" Tundra rolled her eyes and walked over.

She placed her tray on the rectangular table beside the mammoth football player's tray. He lifted his large square head and locked eyes with the tiny teenager. The conversation at the table died down and the high school's linemen focused on their unwanted guest.

"The Dunnes, you're back. What can I help you with?" Tommy Lest, a six foot two, two hundred and fifty pound guard asked. His left cheek bulged outward, stuffed with the low grade meat.

"You can give us our seats back," Tundra suggested.

"Oh, them were your bags?" Tommy pointed over his shoulder at the bags placed against the wall. "Yeah, that's not happening," he smirked.

"You know how hard it is to get a seat in this cramped room," another jock, Brian, chimed in.

"That's why we put our bags on the chairs," she growled.

"Besides we always eat at this table," Tommy informed them. "Grab another seat."

"You can't claim a table," Mac shot back.

"And what were you doing?" Brian countered.

"Mac," a curly redheaded jock called out. "How about you get your mom to stand up for you?"

"Fuck you, Chuck," Mac countered. "She pulled us out to protect your bitch ass."

Chuck stood up showing off his thick six foot frame. "I ain't that little freshman anymore. I will fuck you up now."

"You still whining about what happen two years ago?" Timber inquired.

"The little fucker broke my arm," Chuck reminded everyone. "Ruined my chance to make All Ohio as a freshman."

Tommy stood up and grabbed his friend's Letterman jacket. "Don't man," he warned his friend. "It was an accident. Besides, you'll crush that kid."

"This has escalated fast," Timber whispered to Tundra.

"You fucking kidding me Tommy?" Mac shook his head and placed his tray down on the nearest table. "I will flatten all you fuckers."

"We should just get another table," Cassie tugged on Mac's shoulder.

"Yeah," Chuck pointed at her. "Listen to your snow white bitch. Move the fuck on."

"Wow," Cassie looked to her sister. "Did he just..."

"Yep," Tundra nodded.

"I was looking forward to the blueberry crumble," Cassie put her tray down on a nearby table.

"Oh, it was good," Timber assured her.

A crowd formed, drawn in by the shouts and vulgar language.

"Oh snap," a voice called out from the encircling crowd of students. "The Dunnes done done it now!"

Timber turned to face the crowd. "Shut up Bernard Barnard. I know that was you! Your name is stupid, someone should slap your parents!"

"Got your girls fighting your battles for you, Little Mac?" Chuck provoked.

"What the fuck is your problem, Chuck?" Mac walked over to the curly haired boy.

"You!"

Chuck swung his left arm out. Mac ducked and drove his right fist into the aggressor's ribs. He heard a pop and the kid gasped, the air driven from his lungs. Chuck fell to his knees and Mac delivered a quick left hook to his jaw.

"OOOOHHHHHH!" The crowd groaned.

Chuck fell back unconscious. His teammates rushed to his defense. Timber sidestepped a charging boy and grabbed his jacket. Timber fired two quick jabs at his head. The kid slumped under the onslaught and Timber released him.

Tommy grabbed Tundra's shoulder. She grabbed his hand, pulled him off of her, and twisted his arm. He groaned against the pain. A lightning quick shot to his throat buckled his knees.

Cassie kicked Brian's knee. The giant, howled in pain and grabbed his leg. She pulled her right arm back and swung. Brian never saw the blow that sent him crashing to the floor.

"Break it up!" Mr. Stines shouted and jumped into the fray.

Tundra and her siblings stepped back. Sprawled out before them half the jocks writhed and screamed in anguish. Her heartbeat slowed and their situation became very clear. Shame quickly replaced the anger that flowed through her veins seconds ago.

"Dammit!" She yelled.

1:40PM

Jamila stared at her reflection on the thick glass doors of the police headquarters. She spent several minutes in the parking lot removing mascara smudges from under her eyes. Now she stared at puffy red eyes, content that she was able to get the tears to stop rolling for the moment. Resigned, she pulled open the glass doors.

A rush of cold air greeted her first steps. Her heels clicked against the tiled floor. The walls were painted a stark white, a long wooden desk cut the room in half, separating the public from offices and jail cells set up beyond the lobby.

Behind the desk stood two women preoccupied with paper and computer work. The lobby was empty, the small town not much for drama. Jamila approached the desk. She unfortunately knew both women by name. Sarah, a veteran of the gulf war, was a petite black woman with short hair. Emily stood tall with a slender build and strawberry blonde hair. She joined the force three years ago, just as Jamila's kids' hormones kicked into high gear.

Emily noticed Jamila first and grabbed a clipboard with papers she had set aside earlier. She put on a smile, but notice the haggard look etched on Jamila's face. Her smile faded. "Sarah," she called out.

Sarah looked up from her computer and saw Jamila. She picked up the phone beside the computer. "I'll get Joel," she said.

Jamila approached the desk and plopped her purse down on the desktop.

She cleared her throat and made eye contact with the young officer. "Hi Emily." Her voice was raspy from yelling on her cell phone to a co-worker while on her way to the station.

"Jamila, hi."

Jamila didn't like the sound of pity in Emily's voice, but knew the girl couldn't help it. It also made her afraid of what was next. Emily handed her the clipboard with a pen. She took the clipboard into her shaky hands and let out a long breath to control her emotions. Sarah hung up the phone and moved over to the emotional mother.

"The kids will be out here shortly," she said.

Jamila nodded and began signing the papers. She needed no directions, this wasn't her first time signing these papers. Her hands continued to shake and Sarah reached out and covered Jamila's hand with hers. Jamila shut her eyes. "Are they pressing charges?" She asked.

"Yes," Sarah answered.

Jamila dropped the pen and clutched Sarah's hand. Her eyes shut, her face riddled with wrinkles of concentration as she fought the wave of frustration that poured over her. She opened her eyes to concerned faces.

"Are you okay?" Emily asked.

"How long do I have with them?"

"Well, since you are a social worker they are allowing you to keep custody of your kids," Sarah explained. "You have to show up to court on Monday morning, nine a.m."

"Monday? That gives us only a weekend."

"Yes, the Judge wants to get this started soon. They've been given many breaks so far, but this is too extreme."

"It was that bad?"

"Very, they hospitalized four kids. Possibly ended a couple of their chances at a scholarship. Their parents are very angry. Your kids are being charged with aggravated assault."

"Aggravated assault? But they only ever defend themselves. And weren't these kids like twice my children size?"

"Yes, but witnesses said Mac threw the first punch."

"Dammit, Mac" Jamila folded her arms.

"Jamila, I know this is hard to hear. We both know how much you love these kids, and they love you too. Just try to make these few days special, okay?"

Jamila unfolded her arms and signed her name on the last page. She placed the pen on top of the papers and handed the clipboard back to Emily. The door to her left opened and a large man, Officer Joel Lithgow, stepped out. He held the door open and her four babies walked out with their heads down.

"I will," Jamila said to Sarah.

The kids sat on a bench against a wall. Jamila stopped just before reaching them. They looked pitiful before her. She could tell they'd been crying. Maybe the gravity of their situation has begun to finally dawn on them. Jamila couldn't understand why kids as smart as them still needed to fail to understand.

She cleared her throat. Their heads raised up and finally laid eyes on her. She read their faces. Saw Cassie's face twist in sorrow. Jamila turned her eyes to the officer that led them out. She didn't want their pain to weaken her anger.

Joel gave Jamila a sympathetic nod.

"Car," she said sternly.

The kids rose up off the bench and walked past their mother. She kept her eyes forward and crossed her arms. Her hands squeezed her elbows to hold herself back from either hugging her children or slapping them.

She wasn't sure which she was feeling.

The footsteps were followed by the sound of the large glass door opening and closing. Jamila dropped her head. Joel walked up to the emotionally drained mother.

"Jamila?" He called out to her.

"What, Joel?"

"If you have any trouble with those kids..."

"Excuse me?" Jamila's head snapped up.

"Jamila, I know you love them, but those kids are dangerous. If you saw what they did..."

"Those kids are mine, and I've never had a problem with them. If everyone could stop provoking them maybe they wouldn't be in here all the damn time."

Jamila turned away from him and stormed out of the station. Outside the building she could see her kids gathered around her car. Tundra stood next to the front passenger's door. Walking down the sidewalk to her car Jamila shook her head.

"Tundra, I don't want you in the front," she ordered.

"What?" A crestfallen Tundra responded.

"You heard me," Jamila confirmed. "Timber, get in the front."

Timber's eyebrows raised up. He moved cautiously around the car. He reached out and touched his sister's arm as they passed one another. Once he reached the passenger door, Jamila unlocked the doors and the teens climbed in.

Several minutes passed without a single word being spoken. Mac sat in the seat behind his brother. Beside him Cassie laid her head on his shoulder. Occasionally she would sniff, but her eyes were now dry.

Tundra sat behind their mother. Her legs pulled up to her chest, she leaned against the door and stared out the window.

Mac's eyes shifted to his mother. Her hands gripped the steering wheel so tightly he could see the veins strain. He felt the weight of her anger and sadness weighing the car down. It was suffocating.

"They took our seat," fell out of his mouth.

Cassie lifted her head off his shoulder. Her blue and green eyes glared at him. Timber rolled his eyes and Tundra closed hers.

"So you put them in the hospital?" Jamila snapped back.

"Chuck kept talking," he continued to speak out of necessity. Cassie elbowed him.

"The hospital, Mac," her voice became louder and higher. "You know what that means?"

The car was silent.

"Assault. The kind they will lock you up over. Can't classify this as kids being kids. You ruined their lives and ours."

"Lock us up?" Timber asked.

"I had to argue with my boss to get this weekend with you guys," she wiped at her eyes. "Monday, I don't know what the judge is going to do. I just know he's tired of seeing us."

"I'm sorry Mama," Tundra spoke up. "I should've listened to Cassie."

"Mac, why didn't you just walk away? Why did you have to hit him?"

"He swung at me," Mac explained.

"They said you hit him first," Jamila growled.

"Because he missed hitting me," Mac recalled.

"And Tundra," Jamila looked back through the rearview mirror. "You're supposed to keep this from happening."

"I'm sorry," Tundra apologized. "It got out of hand quick. I should've stopped them, but I..."

Tundra began to cry and Jamila shook her head. Timber reached out and took his mother's arm in his hand. His touch, warm and strong, helped her relax and take a deep breath.

"I'm sorry Tundra. I'm not putting all of this on you."

"It's okay," she muttered.

Jamila reached out to Timber and squeezed his shoulder. Their eyes locked for a moment and he smiled at her.

"Maybe you can run."

"Where?" Timber asked. Her idea took him by surprise.

"Away from here. They'll put you in separate detention centers, all of you, you understand," Jamila squeezed the steering wheel as her mind ran wild with unwanted scenarios.

"They'll find us in a minute," Timber explained.

"No, you can disappear. I don't want them to separate you. I remember the fits you four pulled when apart."

"We were babies then. We've spent nights apart before," Tundra placed a hand on her mother's other shoulder. She could feel the desperation in her mother's body.

"This is different."

"It is, but it's temporary," Timber chimed back in. "If we run and we are caught, they still separate us. We run, and we can no longer see you. That sounds no different than a jail cell. This way, we serve our time, and afterwards we have our whole lives together as a family."

"You're right," Jamila conceded with a sigh. "Okay. What do you guys want to eat tonight?"

The car was silent as the kids looked to one another.

"Come on," Jamila encouraged. "Whatever you want. If we don't have it in the house we'll go and get it."

"Anything?" Mac asked.

"Anything, sweetie. We are going to enjoy this weekend."

"Because it's our last?" Cassie asked.

"Don't talk like that Cassie. Like your brother said, this is only temporary. We'll be together again soon."

"I like spaghetti," Tundra said.

"Me too," Cassie added.

"Spaghetti! There we go. Anybody want to see a movie? What's coming out this weekend?"

"Some cartoon about a horse," Timber answered.

"I don't want to see a cartoon," Mac scuffed.

Jamila turned on to their street.

"We don't have to see a cartoon," she assured him. "We can see anything that is out."

"Cool."

She pulled into the driveway. The car's doors slammed shut behind them and Tundra immediately wrapped her arms around her mother's waist.

She buried her face into Jamila's shoulder and squeezed.

"I'm so sorry," she said, her words muffled.

Jamila leaned back and took Tundra's head in her hands. She wiped tears from her daughter's cheeks and locked eyes with her.

"Do not be sorry Tundra. I love you and this was not your fault. Do you understand?"

Tundra didn't sense a change in her mother's tone or body. "Yes," she answered.

Jamila kissed her daughter's forehead. Tundra rested her head back on her mother's shoulder. Her other siblings joined in for a large group hug. Tundra peeled away after a moment while Jamila kissed each of them in turn.

Turning around she noticed the large white van, from this morning, was now parked in front of their house. Tundra stepped onto the walkway. She looked back over her shoulder to see her Mom with the others in tow.

"We getting our ducts cleaned too?" Cassie asked.

"No," Jamila answered. "Will you guys forget about that van?"

Tundra turned her attention back to the front door only steps away. The van's side door slid open and stopped with a loud thud. The noise caught her attention and she turned. A flash from a rifle surprised her. She looked down to see a dart protruding from her stomach. The feeling in her legs disappeared and her body collapsed against the stone walkway.

Her head throbbing, eye sight fading, and her limbs failing; Tundra fought to remain conscious. She blinked hard to clear her sight, but to no avail. Muttering voices and footsteps sounded miles away. A pair of boots appeared near her feet. She fought the fog in her mind to remember who was behind her. *Mommy*. She urged her limbs to move as the world grew darker around her. A loud pop cracked through the fog. Tundra's mind screamed.

2:50PM

Thomas Banner, a thirty-seven year old detective with deep ebony skin, stood in the doorway of the Dunne's white two-story single family home with blue accents. Gray skies hovered over him. Around the house, just beyond the yellow caution tape, a small crowd formed. Light rain, accompanied by an occasional roll of thunder, dampened their hushed whispers and soft cries to his ears. Officers' wet ponchos, peppered in amongst the crowd, gleamed under the emergency lights, providing counsel and squeezing those willing to talk for any information.

He glanced at his stainless steel watch. He wanted to make sure the body was removed before the school buses began their rounds. He absentmindedly rubbed the cuff of his suit sleeve. Some irrational part of him felt self-conscious about his choice in attire. Of course the day he decided to pull out his black suit would be the day he got his first homicide in five months. His decision to wear it today was triggered by a throw away compliment his wife gave him the last time he wore it, at his uncle's funeral. Decked out with a matching black shirt, tie, and sunglasses; he felt like a mortician surveying the lugubrious scene.

The aluminum joints of a stretcher clicked into place, the noise alarmingly louder than he was used to. It took the crowd by surprise too, silencing them, rain popped against the black plastic body bag. Their eyes, like his, were drawn to the black bag strapped to the stretcher by two thick orange belts. Its wheels creaked against the stone walkway, changing to a low rumble as they hit the asphalt of the driveway. Two EMTs stopped at the back of the ambulance, parked behind Jamila's blue Subaru. Taking their position beside the stretcher they lifted it into the truck, jumped in and shut the door behind them. The ambulance rolled gently out of the driveway and drove down the street slowly.

Banner stepped back into the house, which was filled with noise as every cop in the small town appeared to be stuffed inside the once private home. A weird excitement hung in the air. The last murder in Evansville was between a drug addict and his dealer. The circumstances surrounding this, unfortunately, appealed to everyone's inner detective.

The foyer directed him into the living room. The caramel colored carpet appeared stain free. He found that odd and wondered how she managed that with four rambunctious kids. A fireplace was built into the wall across from him. Between him and the fireplace was a white couch and loveseat facing one another. A rectangular coffee table sat between the two on top of a burgundy circular rug. Two end tables bordered the couch with identical white shaded lamps on each.

Banner took a seat on the couch. Sport and celebrity magazines sat in the center of the coffee table alongside a black photo album. He slipped on a pair of latex gloves and placed the photo album in his lap. He skimmed through the photos, recognizing the in-state amusement parks and some of their other stops. In every picture everyone gave huge smiles. In several shots the kids practically had their mother smothered amongst them.

He shut the book and headed into the dining room. The carpet transitioned into a deep green as he passed through the doorway. Fake plants and trees were shoved into every corner. Photos of big cats dotted the walls and in the middle of the room stood a large black table with six chairs around it. Brown painted walls gave the room a safari feel. To his left was a staircase leading upstairs. He could hear the shuffling of cops working above him. Hands in his pockets, he headed up the stairs.

Photos of the kids growing up followed him up the staircase, from the first day at her old home, the day they moved into town here nine years ago, and each school year after. The photos abruptly stopped halfway up the stairs. He stared at the last set. The kids stood together with tiny US flags in their hands. Around them were crowds of people holding identical flags, kids on shoulders, and a hot dog for everyone. The crowds faced the opposite direction, focused on something other than the camera Jamila held. It dawned on him it was the annual Fourth of July parade the city held. The photo was just a couple of months old. He stared at the blank wall leading the rest of the way up. She expected more memories.

The top of the stairs opened up to a long hallway with five doors, two on each side and one at the far end. Banner entered the first room, the boys' room. Posters of the Cleveland Browns and bikini clad girls dressed the walls. A bunk bed stood to his right with a desk pressed into the far right corner. To his left stood a bookcase; an officer busied himself by flipping each book to check for hidden letters. Along the left wall was the closet where another officer went through the clothes and shoe boxes. Clothes that weren't hung up were scattered across the floor along with a football and soccer ball.

Banner stepped back out into the hallway and headed to the room across from the boys' room. He was taken aback to see Joel seated at the end of a king sized bed with vanilla colored comforter set and pillows. In Joel's hand was a photo of Jamila holding a young Tundra in her arms.

The heavy set officer sat with his head down, grief stricken.

"Joel, what are you doing?" Banner's eyebrows arched.

Joel didn't answer. His eyes were glued to the photo.

"Joel," Banner called out louder.

Joel's head jerked at the sound of his name.

"I warned her about them," he recalled, still entranced by the photo.

"Them who?" Banner didn't like Joel being in here. Everyone knew he doted over the victim. "The kids?"

"They're a fucking menace, Thomas," Joel's red eyes finally connected with Banner's.

"We don't know if they did this."

"How do you not know? They ran. If they're not responsible then why the fuck would they run?"

"Maybe because someone had a gun? We have reports of a strange van sitting in the neighborhood for days."

"Did you see what they did to those boys?" Joel jabbed the air at Banner with the photo.

"No," Banner shrugged his shoulders.

"How can a girl do that to someone twice her size? How?" Joel shook his head as if he were trying to shake the answer loose.

"Joel, you cannot be here. You are clearly not thinking rationally."

"Those kids are on something. Meth?" He looked up to the ceiling. "Something, I don't know." Joel stood up. "I don't understand. They make no sense. What are they?!"

"Who the fuck is yelling?" Phillip Pierre, Banner's partner, asked. He stepped out of Jamila's closet with a box in his hand.

"Joel," Banner answered with a sigh of relief. "He's just about to head back to the station."

"Excuse me," Joel asked.

"Someone has to monitor the influx of information that's bound to come in," Banner said, hoping the man would take the hint.

Joel grumbled, but made his way to the door.

"Picture," Banner ordered.

Joel gave the photo one last look and handed it over. Banner stepped aside and let the man by. He watched the man stomp down the steps and out of sight.

"What the hell was that?" Phillip asked. He opened a folder he had retrieved from the box in his hand.

"The man loves hard," Banner commented and joined his friend at the dresser against the wall.

"Didn't know they had a thing going."

"Yep," Banner smiled. "He asks her out, she says no, and he fantasizes about the day she caves and says yes." Both men chuckled. Banner tapped the box. "What's in the box?"

Phillip's smile broaden at the question. "Medical papers, my friend, you are safe."

"That's good," Banner pulled out a folder with 'Timberland Dunne' on the label. "What does it say?" He asked and opened the folder.

"Yes, my four years at Harvard Med has not been a waste," Phillip dumped his own folder back into the box. "I don't know. It says detective in front of my name, dude, not doctor."

"An unseen genetic manipulation of Myostatin secretion." Banner read out loud. "Myostatin? You heard of it?"

"You just tune me out don't you?"

"I can't listen to every sarcastic thing you say Phil," Banner shut the folder and stuffed it back in the box. "Get this labeled and in my car. This might explain, if the kids did go nuts, why they would."

"You think it was the kids who did this?"

"My gut says no, but I also don't know who else would do this to her."

"What about the Gleason and Forty Fifth boys? Didn't her kids get in a fight with them over the summer?"

"That's the rumor, but the Forty Fifth boys are just vandals and taggers. They haven't escalated, yet. Phil, get the box taken care of and check out the Forty Fifth."

"Alright. Tommy, I'm on it," Phillip took the box in his arms and headed out of the room. "By the way I like your outfit, fits the situation," he called back over his shoulder before disappearing from Banner's line of sight.

Banner looked at his suit and felt self-conscious again. "You dick," he muttered.

4:23PM

Her head throbbed against the cold concrete. She rolled onto her side, felt the restraints tug at her wrist and ankles. The steel clacked together, waking her ears to her new surroundings. She could hear two individuals breathing nearby. Her eyes opened, drawn to her restraints. Two pairs of long chained handcuffs were wrapped around the loop of a massive steel eye bolt cemented into the floor. A black boot stepped into her line of vision. The image of boots approaching her made the vision her mother flash in her mind. She sat up rigid; a man with wide shoulders and a barrel chest wrapped in Kevlar faced her.

"She's up," he said. A black helmet sat atop his head, its chin strap tightly secured. Large goggles hung around his neck and bounced as he talked. "Sedatives wearing off."

"I can see that," the second voice responded in a matter of fact tone.

The second man wore a long white coat. He nonchalantly sat back in an aluminum chair, a clipboard loaded with papers in his lap. His thin grey hair stretched across the top of his balding head, tanned skin etched with stress-induced wrinkles.

The Kevlar man walked away from the scientist to a bed on the opposite end of the room. He picked up a black rod a yard long with two prongs at the end. As he walked back, she noticed the side arm strapped to the man's waist. He took position to her right, her eyes tracking his every movement.

"Do you remember me?" The man in the chair asked.

Tundra turned her attention to him. Her eyes met his curious blue eyes.

She shook her head, no.

The man's mouth curled in disappointment and his eyes went back to the clipboard. He flipped through a few pages.

"I see they call you Tundra," he looked back at her. "I can see how they made that mistake. The species' region was stitched into your clothing.

Your birth name is Dorothy."

"Dorothy?" Tundra repeated.

"I'm very disappointed you do not remember me. I was sure if you didn't recognize the face, my scent would surely trigger your memories. Perhaps you were too young to remember."

"Who are you? Where am I? How do you know my birth name?" Tundra sputtered.

The man placed the clipboard on the floor and walked over to Tundra. He knelt just out of her reach.

"Sir," the guard warned and gripped the rod in his hands more tightly.

The scientist raised his hand to hold back the guard.

"You are so beautiful," he spoke softly.

Tundra scooted backwards. Her chains clanked, preventing further movement.

"We thought we lost you four forever. I am Dr. Luthor Plum. You were named after my aunt. Dr. Porter and I are good friends. He gave me the honor of naming you."

"Why? Did you deliver us or something?"

"Or something."

"I don't understand," she looked at her shackled wrists and ankles.

"Why this? Why kidnap us? Where is my mom?"

"Questions, questions," Plum stood up and sat back in his chair. "These precautions were taken for our safety and yours. Your brothers and sister are in rooms similar to this one. Once we are done taking samples you will be reunited with them."

"And my mom?"

"Your mother is not here."

His words brought back the image of the boots in front of her. The murky pop as she faded into unconsciousness. She shook the image away.

"No, you didn't," she shouted.

The guard stepped forward, but Dr. Plum raised a hand to hold the man at bay.

"We had no use for her."

"What?" Tundra felt her heart sink, and her body began to shake.

"She did well, hiding you. Paying doctors under the table. Kept your records off the radar. Luckily for us one of those doctors could not hold your secret any longer. Once we had him, he spilled all he knew. Your mother was smart, but she was not willing to close loose ends. The Tamberlanes' do not hesitate to close loose ends."

"Fuck you!"

Tundra lunged at the man. The chains caught on the four inch thick bolt and her body crashed against the floor. The guard stepped in quickly, jabbing the rod into her gut. A high pitched whine emanated from the device and currents of electricity, enough to render a cow unconscious, locked her body in a grimace. The guard stepped back. Her body relaxed and she let out a scream.

Plum stepped forward with a syringe in hand, and knelt to deliver the sedative. He took her arm and placed the needle against her skin. The prick startled the teen, and she grabbed his arm and pulled the doctor downward while pulling herself up at the same time. The guard stepped forward. Tundra took the helpless doctor's head in her hand and drove his face into the concrete between her legs. The sound of his skull cracking echoed in her mind.

She noticed the world around her slow down considerably. Blood slowly seeped from the doctor's fractured skull. The chains looked different, more defined, each link moved almost rhythmically to her. Her hands wrapped around the chain and pulled. The restraint snapped easily, tiny fragments reflecting the fluorescent lights above. The guard's foot stomped down a couple feet away from her. The sound echoed; she realized she could hear his heartbeat buried beneath his primal yell. She stood up, watched his momentum carry him closer, grabbed the menacing rod and pulled the man towards her. She spun around, forcing the guard past her. The chain holding her ankles caught on the bolt and snapped.

She stood before the guard, free, with the electric rod in her hands. She smiled. Her heart pounded and she could feel the blood coursing through her veins. She never felt so alive, so in control, in all her life. All her senses appeared to meld slowing her world down, and now she felt no obstructions. The sound of the man's racing heart, the scent of fear in his sweat, and her vision capturing his every movement, every detail as if she was watching an instant replay of her favorite sport play. A new sensation built up within her core, a power, coiled like a spring.

The guard's hand twitched to his side arm. Tundra unleashed a roar from her chest, her leg shot out like a piston, and caught the guard in his chest before his hand could reach the gun. The blow sent him off his feet, blood sputtering from his mouth, and he sailed through the air. He slammed into the wall. Dust and dirt leapt up as his body cratered the thick slab of concrete, and he crumpled to the floor.

Her ears twitched; footsteps at the door. With two powerful strides she covered the length of the room. A smile stretched across her face as the door creaked open.

"Tundra?" A deep voice called out.

The door opened wider and revealed an anxious Mac, his eyes dark pools of rage. She enveloped her brother in her arms. They held each other for a sweet moment.

"I thought I lost you," she finally spoke.

They could feel one another's heartbeats. The familiarity and closeness drained their collective rage. Their muscles relaxed and the knot of energy in their core dissipated.

Mac broke off the hug and stepped back. He locked eyes with his sister. Her pupils constricted back to their normal size revealing their hazel color once more.

"Are you okay?" He asked.

"Yes, your eyes are back to normal."

"Ditto for you too."

"My God, your arm!"

Mac lifted his right arm, caked in blood. Flashes of the doctor and guard's cratered heads shook the frightened child. He tugged at his shirt revealing two burnt holes in the center.

"They stuck me with a cattle prod. I just lost it, everything slowed down, and I couldn't stop..." his throat tightened and he tried to wipe the dried blood off his arm with his other hand. "I killed them... I didn't... I wanted..."

"I know," she squeezed her brother's shoulder.

Mac noticed the two bodies on the other side of the room and moved to them.

"Did you kill them?" He asked, approaching the crumbled guard's body. "I don't know," Tundra focused her attention on her shoes.

Mac stood between the two bodies. He moved to the man in the lab coat.

"The guard is dead," he announced. "But this guy is still breathing, barely."

He noticed the clipboard beside the pool of blood. He scooped it up and took notice of the name at the top.

"Who's Dorothy?" He asked, returning to his sister's side.

"Apparently, the words stitched into our clothing when we were found were not our names."

"Good," Mac dropped the clipboard. "I hated Mackenzie for a boy's name."

"Come on, we have to make sure the others are okay."

She led her brother into the brightly lit hallway. Surprised their escape hadn't triggered any alarms, they moved swiftly and quietly to the next door in line. Tundra opened the door and stepped inside.

"Tell me!" Cassie was shouting.

Tundra and Mac took the scene in. Cassie held another man in a lab coat against the wall by his throat. Her rage echoed in every order she barked out. Sickening thuds of her fist pounding into the tenderized torso of the doctor shook them.

"Where is she?" She shouted.

The man's eyes bobbed with each strike. Blood oozed from his mouth and ran down his chin, coating the back of Cassie's hand. She struck him again.

"Tell me!" Tears rolled down her red cheeks.

Her siblings rushed her. All four bodies fell to the ground in a heap. Mac pushed the doc's lifeless body off of them and immediately he and Tundra wrapped Cassie in their arms. Cassie wept loudly and strained to get at the man lying beside them.

"No! He has to tell me!"

"She's not here!" Tundra shouted.

Her sister's pain became hers, and tears began to blur her vision. Cassie cried out, while Mac ran a hand through her hair.

"She's home," Tundra spoke softly into her sister's ear, their wet cheeks pressed together.

"They left her?" Cassie asked, between sobs.

"Yes, take deep breaths."

Cassie obliged and Tundra could feel her sister's elevated heart rate subside. They jumped, as a loud screech echoed in the hallway. A thud resounded and they clambered to their knees. A familiar smell alleviated their fears and Timber's small frame wandered into the room. His hand clasped the eye bolt that once held him, to the floor. Concrete still clung to the shaft of the bolt. Blood stained the concrete with clumps of hair embedded on it.

He dropped the tiny bolder in front of his siblings. They looked at the bolt and back into his black eyes. Veins protruded along his body. He collapsed to his knees and they rushed to him.

"Deep breaths," Cassie ordered, her arms wrapped around his neck, their chests smashed together.

He exhaled deeply into her ear. Her heartbeat was comforting. The warmth of his family engulfing put him at ease.

"We have to get out of here," he said, back to normal.

"I can hear voices," Tundra alerted everyone.

They could all hear the discovery of Mac's work down the hall and rushed out of the room. The hallway empty, they jogged away from the noise. Tundra, trailing her siblings, looked back in time to see a man step outside the room that had held her.

"There they are," he shouted.

"Run!" Tundra ordered.

The four sprinted, wind whistling in their ears. A shot from a rifle rang out. The hallway came to an end and split off to both sides. They dove right, as a dart smacked against the wall.

"Damn, those fuckers are fast," a man shouted behind them.

"Why are they shooting darts at us like we're fucking animals?" Cassie asked, her voice high with excitement.

"This day is beyond fucked up," Timber groaned.

"There!" Mac pointed to a window down the hallway.

They rushed to it. Standing under the window, they gauged the height. In the distance, hurried footsteps became louder.

"What is that? Like fifteen feet?" Mac questioned.

"About that," Timber estimated. "I'll boost you up."

He pressed his back against the wall and bent his knees as if he was in a chair. Interlocking his fingers to create a foothold. Mac placed his foot in his brother's hand. They counted to three and Timber launched his brother at the same time that Mac jumped. He sailed upwards, and it took him less than a second to realize the boost was probably not needed.

"Jesus!" He shouted, his head colliding with the ceiling.

The others cringed at the sound. Dazed, Mac blindly reached out as he fell, and felt a window sill, and grasped it with his fingertips. His body slammed into the wall, but he held on.

"Get it open, they're getting closer!" Tundra warned.

Mac pressed his hand against the frame. The frame cracked and popped free. The glass shifted, but didn't break. He pushed the frame out of the way and crawled through the opening.

"There's no drop!" He announced. "They had us in a basement."

"That's great," Cassie shouted. "Catch me." Timber prepared to launch his sister up. "Not so hard," she cautioned.

Cassie planted her foot in his hands and immediately was launched upwards. Mac caught her arm and pulled her through.

A group of men turned the corner and spotted the last two attempting to escape. In their hands were long single shot rifles, customized for darts. Two men stopped and fired at the teens. The two ducked and the darts sailed overhead.

"Jump!" Tundra shouted.

Timber leapt into Mac's waiting arms, who pulled him through quickly. Once outside Timber stood up, noticed Cassie looking off into the distance.

"Do you hear that?" She asked. Muffled sounds of engines revved in the distance.

Timber turned to focus on Tundra. Mac had her by the arms and was pulling her out through the window when she screamed. Timber grabbed her shirt and both boys yanked her free of the building. Embedded in her back was a dart.

"Not again!" She cried, her words slurred.

"No, stay awake," Mac shouted, and shook his sister.

She blinked a few times. Their eyes locked for a moment. Her eyelids closed and with a deep breath she was out.

"Dammit," Mac gently slapped Tundra's cheek. "Wake up."

"We have a big problem," Cassie alerted her brothers.

They listened to the high whine of engines making their way around the building. In front of them, leading away from the building, was a thick forest. Just beyond the trees they could hear the sounds of the highway.

"Are those dirt bikes?" Timber asked.

"Sounds like it," Cassie answered.

"I got Tundra," Mac declared, he hooked his hands under her arms and lifted her up and over his shoulder.

"Woods," Timber ran towards them. "If we get to the road before they get us, we'll have a chance to flag down some help."

They rushed into the thick trees as five black dirt bikes appeared around the corner. The engines roared and the bikes raced after them.

Timber's heart raced, but this time it was different. The rush of energy did not accompany it, his muscles didn't coil. Instead he felt loose, weak, tired. His legs and lungs burned.

Could it be the sedative? Had it not fully worn off? Maybe that burst he experienced before was a one-time thing.

Bark exploded off the tree just ahead of him. He ran into the cloud of shrapnel. It stung his face like a hundred hornets. He stumbled and quickly gathered himself, urged his feet to keep moving.

"Bullets!" Mac shouted.

Timber looked back over his shoulder. He was surprised to see his brother so far behind him. He looked ahead and saw Cassie several feet ahead. She too showed signs of fatigue, her arms hung low and her feet dragged. Another glance back at Mac, and Timber noticed the boy had taken Tundra off his shoulder and was now carrying her in his arms to shield her from the gunfire. A bike was closing the gap on the exhausted kid.

Timber dug his heel into the soft earth. He spun on a dime and raced back. Bullets smacked against the tree trunks and fertile grounds. Timber noticed a tree split in two, creating a V shape. He raced for the opening, watched his brother pass, and Timber jumped through feet first. He timed the jump perfectly, striking the armed biker in the helmet. The biker flew off the bike and crashed into a tree. Timber smashed into the ground and rolled. The rider-less bike carried on till it collided with a tree.

Timber sprung up onto his knees. His ribs were sore, but he could see his brother carrying on. The ground erupted around him with geysers of dirt produced by wayward bullets. Bark showered him from above. Timber rolled behind another tree and launched himself back onto his feet.

With the bikers' attention on him, he cut left and right to avoid their bullets. He noticed black spots appearing in his vision. His hands shook and he struggled to suck in air to his burning lungs. He stumbled over an exposed tree root and struggled to regain his balance. The high pitched roar of the dirt bike's engine consumed his senses and he waited for that bullet to strike him down.

The ground gave way beneath him and he fell into Cassie's arms. The engine roar passed over their heads. Timber listened as a man's screams were drowned out by the sound of tires screeching and metal colliding with metal. Several more dirt bikes flew over the hidden ditch and into the I-70 traffic.

"I thought we lost you," Cassie whispered breathlessly into Timber's ear.

"It's not done yet," Mac countered.

Timber rolled off his sister and found themselves staring at a lone biker. The biker had a gun trained on them. A loud screech of rubber against asphalt caught the biker's attention. The biker foolishly fired at the oncoming Honda Civic. It bridged the ditch and slammed into the man.

They crawled out from underneath the car and climbed to the mouth of the ditch to survey the damage. Cassie stared into the Honda to see the driver engulfed in his airbag. Mac dragged Tundra along and left her at the bottom to climb up and see for himself. The scene was worse than all the noise indicated. He counted at least ten cars smashed together. Cries of help echoed throughout. Blood and body parts from the bikers covered the asphalt and some of the cars. One car had a biker hanging through the windshield.

"There's a van," Cassie pointed to a red van idling just outside the pile-up.

Mac turned to get Tundra, only to find Timber already picking her up in his arms.

"I got her for this round," Timber called out.

Mac nodded and they climbed out of the ditch.

4:40PM

Tabitha's hands clutched the steering wheel tightly. Her heart pounded in her ears and she struggled to catch her own breath. Behind her a van-load of seven year old girls, on their way home from a soccer game, vibrated with their high wails. Beside her sat her fourteen year old daughter, Rhonda, who sat frozen, her slim arms outstretched and holding the dashboard in a death grip.

"Rhonda," Tabitha's voice squeaked. "Are you okay?"

"Yes," her daughter's voice quaked.

"Anybody hurt?" Tabitha called back.

She looked into the back. The kids' faces were wet with tears, some held on to their friends, others just look to her for help. None answered her, their nervous sobs too much to overcome. She spotted her youngest, Rebecca, crying.

"Calm down," Tabitha pleaded. "I need you to tell me you're fine. Tell me if you're hurt."

She began to unbuckle her seat belt to check on them herself. Their sobs turned into individual gasps as each child try to regain their composure.

"Mom," Rhonda's voice stopped Tabitha.

She ran her eyes over her daughter. "What is it? Are you hurt?"

"No, there are some kids coming this way," Rhonda pressed a finger against the window.

"What?"

Tabitha looked past her daughter's almond colored hair. The scene reminded her of old war photos from 'Time' magazines. The three kids rushed toward her. They were covered in dirt, and one carried a girl in his arms. In the background was a pile of twisted metal, smoke and blood. She knew right then this image would stick with her forever.

"Oh my god, one of them is hurt," she placed a hand over her mouth.

The girls piled in the back fell silent. Tabitha pulled her hair back and twisted it into a quick bun. She maneuvered her small frame between the two seats and reached the side door just as the teenagers arrived. With a grunt she swung the door open. The boy carrying the girl shoved her into the woman's arms.

"Is she?" She asked, the words caught in her throat, unable to finish.

"No," the boy said sternly. "She's still alive."

He grabbed the girl's legs and lifted her into the van, forcing Tabitha to back up. A girl with white hair and equally pale skin hopped into the van.

"Thank you for letting us in," she said.

"You need help," Tabitha explained. "I couldn't leave you four out there."

The van quickly filled up. Tabitha moved back into the driver's seat. Cassie moved nimbly to take Tabitha's previous position and cradle the unconscious girl's head in her lap. The boys shut the door behind them and settled in.

"You have to get us to the Evansville Police Station right away," the girl pleaded.

"Police station?" Tabitha looked back at the unconscious girl. "We need to get her to a hospital."

"She's just asleep," the girl informed her. "They tranquilized her."

"They what?"

"No time to explain. You have to take us now!"

"I am taking her to the hospital, she needs a doctor!"

One of the boys moved quickly between them. His face just inches from hers, she found herself fixated by his light green eyes. He put his fist between him. She finally noticed the blood-stained handcuff locked to his wrist. The chain dangled down his forearm, broken.

"They chained us and we broke free. Some of their bodies are splattered all over this highway, but they're going to send more. We need protection, not a doctor."

His words came out calm and soft. Tabitha nodded and settled back into her seat. She put the car in drive and pulled away from the wreckage.

The car was quiet for most of the ride. Rhonda would periodically look into the back to survey their guest. Something seemed familiar about them. It dawned on her while staring at the white hair girl who ran her fingers through the sleeping girl's hair.

"Oh shit," she exclaimed, shattering the silence.

"Rhonda, language," Tabitha snapped.

"You're the Dunne kids," she clasped her hands together pleased she solved the mystery on her own.

"Yeah, so," Mac muttered from the back.

"Oh no," Tabitha whispered to herself.

Their ears caught that, but they were used to parents' aversion to them.

"Everyone heard about that epic fight you had this morning," the words poured out of the teen rapidly.

"Damn, already?" Mac scratched his head.

"That was fast," Timber commented, his voice soft, exposing his weariness.

"What time is it?" Cassie asked.

Tabitha glanced at the clock in the dashboard.

"It's five oh five."

"Wow, they had us for a long time."

Cassie leaned back and rested her head against the side of the car. She peered down at her sleeping sister. She couldn't wait for her to wake up.

"Your hair is pretty."

Cassie looked up to see a small black girl smiling at her, her hair braided with purple clips at the ends. She reached out with her little brown hand and touched Cassie's hair.

"Thank you," Cassie gave a weak chuckle. "I like your uniform."

All of the little girls were wearing soccer uniforms resembling a bumble bee.

"Rebecca, get them something to drink out of the cooler," Tabitha called back to her youngest daughter. "You poor kids sound exhausted."

"Thank you," Cassie said.

Mac watched as a small blonde girl sitting behind him reached into the back. She came back with juice in silver pouches. She handed them to Mac, who took them with his clean hand and made sure to hide the blood encrusted arm from her view. He distributed the drinks to his siblings.

The surge of liquids energized their bodies. Done with their first pouch, they asked for seconds. The girls obliged and they felt their strength returned.

Mac surveyed the group of tiny bumblebees. The girls were enamored with the unexpected arrivals and appeared to have forgotten about their narrow escape earlier. One tiny girl reached out and took a fistful of Mac's hair and squeezed it. His mass of hair a source of wonder to her young eyes.

Mac pulled his head away from her tight grip. "Who are you guys? The Evansville Bumblebees?"

"Banbury," Rhonda answered for the girls, peering over her seat into the back.

"Banbury sucks donkey balls," Mac countered without a second thought.

"Excuse me?" Tabitha interjected. "There are children in this van."

"Sorry," Mac apologized. "Just still antsy." He stared at Rhonda. The girl's auburn hair was curled, and brushed against her soft cheeks. Her large brown eyes stared back at him. "You are cute," he blurted out.

"Oh no," Tabitha grabbed her daughter and forced her to look forward.

"Mac," Cassie tossed her empty juice box at her brother.

"Mom," Rhonda whined.

"What?" Mac looked around, his eyes wide with confusion. "I just said she was cute."

"You are not talking my daughter like that," Tabitha looked at Mac through his reflection in her rearview mirror. "I know who you are and you are too old for her."

"What you know about us?" Mac countered, ignoring Cassie's foot tapping his thigh.

"I was at that homecoming game two years ago," She pointed at Mac's reflection. "You and your brother were ruthless out there. What are you, seventeen now?"

Mac rolled his eyes at the mention of the infamous homecoming game.

"We're fifteen," Mac stated.

"Check that," Timber finally spoke up.

"What you mean check that?" Cassie asked, her hands still stroking Tundra's hair.

"None of you looked at the charts those...," he looked at the children around him. "Guys were carrying?"

"I glanced at Tundra's," Mac shrugged while Cassie shook her head.

"Eighty-five," Timber sighed. "We were born in eighty-five, not eighty-seven like we were told."

"Who made that clerical error?" Cassie asked.

"Man, mama got some explaining to do," Mac pointed out.

"You think they just left her to wake up on the lawn and find us gone?" Timber countered.

Tabitha remembered the text she received from her aunt who lived in Evansville, just a couple hours ago. Her hand gripped the steering wheel. The Evansville exit just ahead, she clicked the turn signal on.

"Sure," Mac said, the click alerted him and he caught sight of the exit sign.

"I hope you're right."

Timber tinkered with the handcuff on his wrist. With his energy back up he hooked his fingers around the steel. He tugged against it. The steel strained and popped off, startling everyone in the van. The handcuff fell into his lap. He eagerly attacked the other and it popped off with little effort. His siblings followed his lead, Cassie ripping Tundra free of her bonds.

The van cruised through the small town. Along Jewel Avenue shops lined both side of the streets. Each building they passed the kids watched intimately. Happy to be home, a part of them couldn't help but feel everything was slightly different. They knew that their arrival, albeit exciting or comforting, was temporary.

5:26PM

Tabitha parked her van in front of the police station's double paned glass doors. The side door slid open and both Timber and Mac jumped out into the rain. Thunder cracked overhead, the kids inside the truck jumped. Timber grabbed Tundra by her ankles and pulled the girl back into his arms with Cassie's help.

"I'm coming in to let them know what happened," Tabitha called to the grimy teenagers.

"That's alright," Cassie said, one leg outside the van.

"No, I'm not leaving you four," she unbuckled her seat belt. "Kids, we're getting out."

The youngsters unbuckled themselves and Tabitha put her eldest in charge of the younger ones. She jumped out the van and ran around it to catch up with the Dunnes. Cassie held the door open for her brothers.

Emily spoke calmly on the phone with unsettled civilians worried about the accident on I-70. Sarah busied herself with keeping track of the units who had rushed out to handle the pile up. The station was virtually empty with the exception of those on desk duty and a few detectives busy with other cases.

They looked up at the sound of the door opening. Emily pulled the phone away from her ear. The kids' muddied and blood stained clothes were in stark contrast to her last image of them. Their wet shoes squeaked across the floor. A blonde woman, and an army of children behind her, followed them.

"What happened?" Sarah dropped what she was doing.

"Is Tundra okay?" Emily asked.

"We were kidnapped," Cassie cried out.

"They tranquilized her," Mac informed the two officers.

"Tranquilized?" Sarah asked.

"Drugged, sedated. Whatever the fuck fits the situation," Timber barked back.

"Okay," Sarah hopped off her chair. "Emily, call Banner. Get him up here."

Emily looked at the phone she still held. Some distant voice still harped away. She hung up the phone and picked it back up to dial Banner's extension. Sarah rushed around the counter to check Tundra's vitals.

The door leading back to the offices opened. Emily looked back, the line to Banner's phone still ringing. She thought it would be Banner, but her heart sank when she saw the heavyset Joel step into the room.

"This is Banner," his voice fell on flustered ears.

"Shit," Emily exclaimed, as she saw recognition ignite in Joel's eyes.

Joel saw the four kids huddled together at the desk. An image of Jamila's body wrapped in a blood stained sheet flashed in his mind. His hand went to his gun, the kids stepped back from the desk sensing the man's rage. He ignored their distraught expressions and tattered clothing. Gun out, he pointed it at the youngsters.

"Hands up, on your knees!" He shouted, his face red.

"What the fuck are you doing?!" Mac shouted back.

"Put it away, Joel," Sarah ordered. She changed directions to place herself between the kids and the enraged officer.

"You're under arrest!" He yelled, moving closer to the startled children.

Tabitha grabbed her eldest daughter and they moved away from the chaotic scene to the front doors. Emily dropped her phone and raced out to assist Sarah. Timber shielded his sister with his body. Cassie and Mackenzie stepped in front of him to shield him.

"Arrested for what?" Mac snapped back.

"Joel, shut up!" Sarah came up beside him and put her hand on his forearm. "They were kidnapped."

"Get off me," Joel shrugged the small woman off him.

"Don't say it," Emily ran up to him and stood directly in front of him.

"What the hell is wrong with you?" He stormed past her. "Don't you see what I'm doing? I told her to watch out for them."

"Check your guy?" Mac yelled at the two women.

"You're fucking insane," Cassie screamed.

"Knees now," he waved his gun to the ground.

The kids stood their ground.

"I fucking said on the ground."

"They're victims," Sarah pleaded.

"Don't you let them fool you."

"Joel," Banner's deep voice echoed in the lobby. "Holster your firearm now!"

Everyone in the lobby froze, the gravitas in his voice demanded it. The phones rang in the sudden silence. He walked over to Joel, grabbed the man by his shoulder and threw him against the wall. He ripped the gun from the stunned man's hands.

"What are you doing?" He growled.

"They killed..."

"You see Joel, this is why you have not been in the field for a year.

You're emotional and you're stupid."

83

"You can't talk to me like that," Joel's eyes dropped to the floor.

"Dammit Joel, you do not pull a gun on kids who walked in here on their own," he noticed tears well up in Joel's eyes. "Wow, okay look, I want you to go home. This case is clearly too personal for you to handle. I don't want you in this building for the rest of the day."

He shoved the man away to the back. Turning around, all eyes were on him. He surveyed the scene and noticed the unconscious girl.

"She's under some kind of sedative," Sarah remarked when she noticed his reaction.

He nodded.

"Get back to the phones," he instructed.

The two returned to their stations. Banner walked over to Jamila's children. He looked over them at the woman and her band of bumblebee children.

"Who are you, ma'am?"

"I'm Tabitha Samite," she stammered and gripped Rhonda's shoulders tighter. "They came to my van after the pile up."

"You were at the crash site?" He looked to Cassie.

"Yes, they had us in some building and were chasing us on dirt bikes and..."

"Hold up," Timber interrupted.

In his arms Tundra stirred. Her eyes fluttered open. She took in her surroundings and jolted upright. She looked up at Timber and placed her hand on his face.

"We're in the police station?" She asked.

"Yes," Timber answered.

"Good," she noticed Tabitha and the kids. "What's with the bees?"

"Alright, Dunnes, I want you to follow me," Banner ordered. He looked over at Sarah. "Contact the officers at the crash site. Have them check out the kids' story about the building. Also get a statement from..."

"Tabitha," The mother clarified.

"Right, sorry. Also get a doctor here to check these kids."

Sarah nodded and headed over to fulfill her task. Banner led the four tired teenagers into the back. Despite their frequent trips to the station, the teens had yet to see this side of the building. Desks were crammed into the center of a massive white walled room with navy blue wall to wall carpeting. A few people occupied desks in the otherwise vacant space. Fluorescent lights hummed overhead, offices lined the far right wall, while three rooms labeled as interview rooms were to the left. Banner turned right and led them to an oak wood door. A name plate beside the door read, 'Detective Thomas Banner'. He opened the door and stepped aside to allow the kids in.

They walked into the windowless, cramped office, with numerous filing cabinets in every corner and a bookshelf opposite the door. A desk, covered in paper and boxes, stood to their right, two wooden frame chairs with worn down fabric cushions in front. Across from the desk was a small gray loveseat, Banner's black blazer draped over it. His wet black trench coat hung on a coat hanger next to the door.

The coat's faded dye suggested age, but the soft aroma, in conflict with the lived in items, told the teens it was new to the office. Nostrils flared as they adjusted to their new surroundings. A photo of Banner's arm wrapped around a dark skin beauty drew Tundra's eyes. The rare smell she and the others picked up on in his clothing clicked in her head. She picked up the photo.

"She's pregnant," Tundra blurted out.

"Yes, how do you know that?" Banner asked, taken aback by the accurate prediction.

Tundra placed the photo back down. "I don't know, a weird smell I always recognize around pregnant women."

"Your clothes reek of it," Cassie added.

"Why do you have something from our mother's room in here?" Timber asked.

Banner's eyes drifted to his desk. The box was behind the desk on the floor, hidden from their view. Timber's discovery and the girl's explanation set off questions in his own head, but their eyes begged for an answer.

"It's evidence in our investigation," he answered.

"Investigation?" Cassie repeated. "Did she bring them in?"

"No," Banner pointed at the chairs in front of his desk. "Take a seat."

His answer mixed with Joel's words in their minds. He watched them connecting the dots. Tundra gasped and braced herself against his desk.

Banner's eyes drifted to the open folders lying there.

"They killed her?" Tundra asked the sounds of boots against the pathway enveloping her.

Banner nodded.

5:48PM

Banner shut the door behind him. He exhaled deeply, never a fan of delivering bad news.

"Detective."

Sarah's voice caught him by surprise. He jumped, and she smiled at his sudden reaction and held up a sheet of paper.

"Tabitha's statement," she handed the paper over.

Banner took the single sheet of paper. It only bared a few paragraphs, nothing more.

"She didn't know a lot," Sarah explained.

"Clearly," Banner agreed. "You hear back from the officers in the field yet?"

"Not yet. They'll let us know if they find anything soon as they can."

Banner looked at the door to his office. The pain in their faces as he told them the news replayed in his mind. Wiping a hand over his face, he knew that image would stick with him. "Did you call social services?" He asked.

"Yes, they're sending someone as we speak. I also called the hospital.

They were able to free up a doctor to check the kids out."

"Thank you, you're a time saver."

The door to his office opened. The four small teenagers stood in the doorway. Their eyes were red, faces puffy.

"We need to wash up," Tundra announced.

"Hungry?" Banner asked.

"Starving," Mac said.

The others nodded. Banner looked out over the center of room. The officers referred to collection of desks jammed in the space as the pit. He didn't see his partner at his desk. "Hey, Phillip," he called out. He looked back at the kids. "What are ya'll in the mood for?"

"Whatever you can get here now," Tundra answered.

Banner pondered her request when Phillip entered from the lobby.

"What's up Tommy?" He asked. "Whoa, it's Jamila's kids!"

"Yeah, I need you to run out and get them something to eat."

"Are they okay?" He noticed their ragged state.

"Doubt it. They're hungry though. I need you to get them some fast food."

"Anything specific?" He asked the kids.

"Burgers, fries, whatever. Just get it here now. We haven't eaten since breakfast," Timber grumbled.

"Right," Phillip jogged away.

"Where's the restroom?" Tundra asked. "I don't want to eat with these," she looked at her stained hands. Clench them in a fist and dropped them to her side. She sighed. "Where?"

Banner pointed the kids to the restroom on the other side of the room.

The two law enforcement officers watched the kids make their way. Satisfied they were heading in the right direction, Banner stepped into his office. He stopped midway and looked over his shoulder at Sarah. The material and information he discovered in their mother's closet weighed on his mind.

"Sarah, don't freak, but I think we are in the middle of something much bigger than a kidnapping case," he told her in a soft whisper.

"What makes you say that?"

"Come in," he stepped to the side to allow Sarah into his office.

Inside the restroom, they listened to make sure they were alone. Satisfied, Tundra locked the door to the women's restroom. The four of them picked a sink and began the process of cleaning themselves. Soaping and lathering over and over, wet hands and drenched forearms.

"We can't stay here," Timberland stated.

"Yeah," Tundra mumbled.

"They'll put us in some temporary home," Mac added.

They rinsed their hands and forearms. Blood and dirt residue remained on their skin. They started the process over again. Wet, soap and lather.

"I know," She countered.. "Besides, whoever took us will find us again."

"Why are they doing this?" Cassie asked.

"I don't know," Tundra admitted. "Dr. Plum, at the facility, mentioned all the times Mommy took us to the doctors. Said that's how they were able to find us. Apparently they knew us since birth. Then they lost us somehow."

"Didn't know you were on a name basis with them," Mac grumbled.

"Well when you let people speak, you learn a thing or two, Mac," Tundra snapped back.

They dipped their hands under the flowing water of their individual sinks. The dirt and blood stained the sinks. They repeated the cycle once more.

"So what else did he say?" Cassie asked.

"Not much," Tundra shrugged, her hands and forearms white from the soap. "He called me Dorothy. I smashed his head into the floor."

"Fuck," Mac exclaimed. He closed his eyes to recall the image of the clipboard. "I should've looked past the first page. Also Dorothy, your birthday is in August."

"Don't call me Dorothy you dick," she gave her brother a kick to his shin.

"Now he remembers," Timber shook his head.

"Sorry," Mac recalled. "You were right about our birth year."

"What about it?" Tundra looked to Timber.

"We share the same birthday. August twenty-sixth, nineteen eighty-five."

They rinsed for the last time.

"Eighty-five? So we're sixteen?" Tundra tried to comprehend the revelation. "We're one odd looking quadruplets."

"We have to get out of here before they put us in some place that'll leave us vulnerable," Cassie reminded them while grabbing enough paper towels for all.

"Well," Tundra mulled over their next move. "We should wait till we eat. We haven't eaten since breakfast and I feel drained."

The others nodded. The rustle of paper against wet skin was the only sound for a moment.

"As long as we stay on the move they can't get to us," she continued. "Once we break free of here, we can figure out how to pay these fuckers back for what they've done. Then we'll find out why."

Banner, seated at his desk, showed the folder with printed out news articles to Sarah. She looked at the two articles. One referred to a Dr. Slaughter, killed in a drunk driving incident. The other, a Dr. Suggs, died in an electrical fire that engulfed his home, killing him and his entire family.

"How did you find this out so fast?" Was the only question that popped in her head.

"This thing called Google," He pointed at his monitor. "Gets you the answers you need."

"So you think the kids got them killed?"

"Well, it's possible that these are just two coincidences, but after today's events you have to wonder. I haven't looked at the other doctors yet, however both of these men were onto something big." He pulled out a piece of paper. It was a copy of notes Dr. Suggs had written.

"Apparently, Ms. Dunne was very curious about her kids' natural gifts. And Suggs found something. He speaks of Myostatin, a protein that limits our muscle mass. The higher the protein, the weaker you are. Lower it and you're superman."

"Which would explain how they snapped steel handcuffs like they were twigs," she placed the articles back on Banner's desk.

"Yes," Banner looked up at the petite officer. "Wait what?"

"It's in Tabitha's statement," Sarah tapped the statement she handed him earlier.

"Oh, right," he placed the doctor's note down and locked eyes with Sarah. "Dr. Suggs describes it as a rare form of Myostatin. Your muscles are supposed to get bigger when there is a low amount in your bloodstream. However, they are tiny kids, but their muscles are very dense. It's why they feel like steel when you touch them.

"Suggs wanted to do more, but Ms. Dunne didn't want her kids to become his personal lab rats. He was going to release a thesis, keeping the kids anonymous. He never got the chance to though."

"And Dr. Slaughter?"

"An ophthalmologist, almost a similar tale. Except he found an abnormality when doing a typical eye exam. I haven't deciphered all the medical jargon in his notes yet," Banner pointed to a pad where he had scribbled words to look up. "Apparently it has to do with their ability to see far distances and at night."

"Night vision?" Sarah crossed her arms. "Is that even possible?"

Banner leaned back in his chair. "He referenced it so I'm going to go with the doc."

Sarah sat on the edge of Banner's desk, leaned close to him and whispered. "And how long did he get to live after making this discovery?"

Banner held up two fingers. "Two months."

The door to his office opened. He shut the folder and watched the four kids walk back into his office. They took their seats. The smell of soap hung in the air.

"Where's the grub?" Tundra asked.

6:27PM EST
THEODORE ROOSEVELT NATIONAL
MEMORIAL PARK, ND

Nathaniel Porter sat in his office, his metallic desk cluttered with papers and folders. Behind the hills of papers, tucked into the far right hand corner of the desk, was his chrome monitor. The monitor displayed thirteen year old data of his greatest creation.

It was the only bit of their research salvaged during the raid twelve years ago. Now he awaited a replay of that terrible night. The unfortunate news of his team's failures had forced him to call the Chief Executive Officer for additional assistance.

He opened a small desk drawer and pulled out a photo. He stared at his family. His wife held their two children, a boy and girl, in her arms. He stood behind them, in the photo, with his long arms wrapped around them. His chin rested on top of her head. He could still smell her long black hair. She smelled of raspberries.

He shut his eyes. He could feel her body against his. Raspberries in the air. His hand reached out and opened a larger drawer. He pulled out a large bottle of Glenlivet single malt liquor. The dull orange liquid shined in the bright lights of his office. He reached back into the drawer and retrieved an old fashioned glass. He set the cup and bottle on the desk. The glass clanged, echoes resounding from his office walls. Filling the glass, the sweet aroma of whiskey filled his nostrils. He sipped from the glass, stared at the photo once more.

Ten years ago was the last time he saw his family. After the raid, and the destruction of their valuable work, the CEO made an example of him. He gave Nathaniel a promotion, Head of Research and Development for Lane Industries, but at a price. The cost was his family. Crushed under a semi-truck, the same night he ushered them out for fear of their safety. He wondered what punishment they would bestow upon him if he failed to retrieve these four kids.

A knock at the door wrenched him from his deep thought. He took a large gulp from his glass and called his assistant Pam in. Pam had worked under him for the past five years. They plucked her from one of the world's leading research pharmaceutical companies. She's been his right hand ever since.

Pam entered the office. Her shoulder length brown hair bounced with each step. Her honey brown skin was darkened by the summer sun. The white lab coat hid the curvy physique that he knew all too well. He locked eyes with her. He noticed her visible reaction to his current state.

"What do you have for me, Pam?" He asked and picked up the whiskey glass. He held it in front of his lips.

Pam tapped the screen on a small electronic pad. "Information from Seattle has come in," she reported.

"And?"

"First and second human trials have completed with no problems.

They're ready to put the project into action."

Porter nodded at the good news. He finished what was left in the glass and poured himself another.

"At least something is going right," he drained the cup empty. "What's the ETA on Tamberlane?"

"Not long," she checked her pad. "Twenty minutes at the most." Porter nodded and poured himself another glass.

"That bad huh?" Pam asked. She never did like to see him drown himself in a bottle.

"You have no idea," he took another drink. "We've dragged you into a world that even I have yet to understand. And if this does not happen the way they want it to..."

The sudden pause left his assistant noticeably unnerved.

"Nate?"

"The Tamberlanes are more than they appear," he absentmindedly ran his finger along the rim of the glass, creating an eerie sound. "They control more than you or I could ever imagine."

"What are you talking about?"

He looked into the woman's eyes, and could feel her unease. Sensed her fear. He shrugged it off, and sat back in his creaky chair. "I'm talking too much. If you're lucky you'll live your whole life without a glimpse behind the curtain. Thank you for the update."

Pam nervously jiggled her leg. "Nathaniel, I..."

"Will you let me know when Douglas arrives?"

"Yes."

The door shut and Porter turned to face his cluttered desk. Staring at the glass of whiskey he decided against another taste. Douglas would arrive soon and he would need his wits about him.

He began to replay the first moment he had met the old man. Douglas was confined to a wheelchair; which he insisted was an old war injury. Porter didn't press the man further on the issue, and now regretted that decision. Perhaps, if the Tamberlanes, were more forthcoming about their goals he would not have gone into business with them. No, he knew his quest to achieve what no other man on earth had ever achieved was too strong at the time. Moments after getting the green light from Douglas he had been up and running. Twenty years later he created four marvels.

Then his eyes were finally opened.

It took his family's deaths to open them. He held up the photo once more. He looked at his little girl Ariel, the only body not found in the wreckage. A part of him believed her to be alive, somewhere safe with another family. He smiled to himself, he could remember her speaking freshly learned Spanish, taught to her by her mother. Little Ariel resembled her mother in every way, from her dark hair to her cinnamon skin tone. The only contribution he made was her large ears.

A knock at the door evaporated his memories. The door cracked and Pam's head appeared.

"Tamberlane is in the building," she alerted him.

He nodded and waited patiently. Several minutes passed before the door opened and in wheeled in Douglas Tamberlane. The old man was still ticking after their nearly four-decade-long partnership. Even back then

Nathaniel had felt Douglas wasn't long for this world. Clearly the Tamberlane bloodline was as resilient as their wallets.

Behind Douglas, faithful and quiet, was his grandson Dwight. His grandson was another prime example of their good genes. In the two-score partnership Dwight had barely aged, with the exception of his graying black hair.

"Twelve years later, and I am feeling deja vu," Douglas' graveled voice cracked with age as he spat out his words.

Nathaniel stood as was customary while addressing the CEO. "The situation has proved difficult," he reported.

"Clearly," Douglas scratched at his pale rugged caramel skin. "You lost them again."

"We can get them back."

"I sure hope so. This was to be a simple recovery mission."

"Yes, sir. That was our expectation as well. We underestimated their fight or flight response. Our efforts to contain them proved insufficient."

"Which is why I am here, correct?"

Nathaniel stared into Douglas' dark eyes. Despite the man's aging body and scarred, saggy skin, his eyes continued to burn boldly through the years. There were years of rage in those eyes, a rage whose origin came long before Porter entered the picture.

"Yes. We need more men and equipment. I feel the only way to conduct our tests is to put them in a medically induced coma."

Douglas' dark eyes roamed the room and stopped at the liquor bottle and photo. His face twisted in a sick grin of satisfaction.

"I don't have to remind you of the consequences if you fail me again," his rage filled eyes found Porter's.

Nathaniel's fingers curled into a fist. "I'm aware," he tried to keep his voice firm.

"Don't drink too much," Douglas cautioned. "What's happening with the project in Washington?"

"The Gridlock Project is ready for Alpha group."

"Good, we'll get them their specimen in few months' time."

"Sir, they're ready to go now," Porter informed him.

"I understand, Nate, but our targets have yet to be acquired and tested. Once we are satisfied we'll move them on to the Gridlock Project," Douglas rubbed the cuffs of his sleeves. He appeared annoyed having to explain simple logic to a scientist.

Porter nodded dutifully. "Yes, sir."

"You focus on your task. Now you have a place for me to send your reinforcements?"

"Yes, our fallback position is in Columbus. A building in the southeast section of town. You can bring them directly through the Rickenbacker Airport. We're only a few miles from there."

"Ah," Douglas nodded his head. The place was familiar. "Back to our old stomping grounds I see."

A knock caught everyone's attention and Pam stepped into the room.

"What is it?" Nate asked.

"They found them, in a police station. They want to know if they should proceed."

"Yes," Douglas answered for Nathaniel. "Nate, I want you there to supervise this. I do not want another failure."

"Yes, Mr. Tamberlane."

7:45PM
EVANSVILLE POLICE STATION

They listened, from inside Banner's office, to the social worker, a doctor, and Banner discuss their next move. The doctor cleared them health wise and the social worker made arrangements to have the kids stay at a foster home for the weekend. Banner wanted an around the clock police presence for their safety. The social worker had no problems due to the circumstances.

"I ain't staying in some stranger's house," Mac grumbled to his siblings.

He took a sip from his 'Biggie' sized cup filled with Dr. Pepper. Bags from Wendy's littered Banner's office. They had Phillip go on a second run to the fast food restaurant after their first helping did little to satisfy their appetite. Now they're scavenging through the bags looking for bottom fries.

"Should we leave now before they take us?" Cassie asked.

Tundra grabbed a couple of loose fries from a bag. She stuffed them in her mouth, tossed the empty bag to the wayside. She shook her head and swallowed the food. "Not yet," she sipped from her cup. "We'll bounce when we are in the car."

"Make a run for it at a red light?" Timberland asked.

Tundra nodded in the affirmative.

"Where do we go from there?" Cassie asked.

"No idea," she admitted. "Probably have to go back to Columbus."

"You think this has to do with how we ended up on the side of the highway?"

"How else you think we got there? You remember the nightmares we had as babies?"

Timber groaned and stood up. "I was afraid they would turn out to be real," he acknowledged and placed his drink on Banner's desk. "You remember where Mama said we were picked up?"

"I think it was..."

The room went dark, and they froze for a second. Their eyes quickly adjusted to the room. The reflective membrane in their eyes caught the soft yellow hue of street lamps outside the office windows. The darkness began to fade and revealed a muted version of Banner's office. Banner swung open the door.

"Stay..." The words he planned to speak left his mind.

In front of him, seated in his office were four pairs of flickering eyes. He tried to gather himself to speak, but all he could muster was a confused groan. Timber walked over to him. His eyes glowed and Banner fought the urge to step back.

"It takes some getting used to," the boy said. "Our eye doctor was shocked to see we have tapetum lucidum membranes."

"Freaked him out so much we never saw him again," Tundra added and stood up.

"I need you four to stay in here," Banner finally said. "The storm must've knocked the power out."

Timber shook his head. "Storm? There's been no thunder for like an hour. It's drizzling outside. It's them."

"I understand you're scared."

"We have to get out of here," Tundra shouted.

"Look, the backup power will come on soon and we'll get you out into a nice home. They're not going to come into a police station."

"They're not afraid of cops," Timber argued. "They gunned down our mother and kidnapped us in broad fucking daylight! They'll gun you down without a thought!"

"Timber, I need you to relax and think. I understand your fears, but you are in a police station. We can protect you."

The backup power clicked on. The open space behind Banner was dully lit by emergency lights. Banner looked to the social worker and doctor who stood idly beside him. He looked back into his office at the nervous teens.

"See, backups are working."

"Sorry," Tundra whispered.

"What?" Banner asked and leaned forward.

Tundra charged at Banner. He never saw someone move so fast and before he could react her shoulder drove into his chest. She felt like a wrecking ball had slammed into him. His lungs compressed and his feet lifted off the ground. Her siblings ran out of the office and raced past the startled social worker and doctor. Phillip watched Banner's body hit the floor from the other side of the room. The kids rushed into the pit.

"Hey, stop!" He shouted to no avail.

Mac led the way through the pit and into the lobby. The startled officer at the front desk, along with a small crowd of civilians still trying to sort out the pile up on I-70, stared in shock as the group of teens tore through the small crowd like bulldozers. An officer positioned himself between the kids and the front doors.

"Stop," he demanded.

Mac drove his shoulder into the hip of the tall lanky officer. Mac's momentum sent the officer somersaulting over him. The crowd gasped in shock. Cassie slipped past her brother and pushed the doors open. They stopped and scanned the parking lot.

"Where?" Cassie called out, her voice hurried.

"Hold on," Tundra held up a pair of keys. She pressed the lock button twice. A faint beep echoed in the misty air.

"You got his keys?" Timberland asked.

"Yep, come on," Tundra ran towards the car.

Banner leaned against the door to the lobby. One arm clutched his sore chest. "Don't let them get out!" He shouted.

"They already got out," Emily stated.

"How the fuck?" Banner mumbled, and proceeded to make his way through the crowd. "Well, don't let them leave the fucking parking lot. We have to protect them."

"I don't think they need much help," an officer picking himself up off the floor said. "What are they made out of?"

Banner shoved his way past the complaining officer. He stepped out into the soft rain. He scanned the parking lot. Phillip joined him. An engine roared to life amongst the resting cars. Headlights flicked on in a familiar spot. Banner quickly patted his empty pockets.

"No," he groaned.

"That's your car isn't it?" Phillip asked.

Across the street, an SUV lights and engine came to life.

"I should be driving," Mac shouted from the back seat.

"Then you should've gotten the fucking keys!" Tundra snapped back.

She scooted up in the seat so her legs could reach the pedals. She shifted the car into reverse and slammed her foot on the gas. The car raced out of the spot and Tundra instinctively slammed her foot on the brake. The tires screeched and slid against the wet asphalt. The kids were jostled around inside.

"Seatbelts, everyone," Tundra shouted.

"I should drive," Mac reiterated, while clipping his seatbelt on.

Secured in her seat Tundra eased the car out the parking space and slowly directed the car out of the crowded parking lot. Timber, next to his brother in the back, looked out the back window.

"Banner is pissed," he revealed to the others. "Shit, we got company. You should probably go faster!"

Tundra looked back. A black SUV pulled off the curb and headed at them.

"Tundra!" Cassie shouted and grabbed the wheel in time to avoid the curb.

Tundra took control and eased the car to the street.

"Faster!" Mac yelled. "Can you even see over the steering wheel?!"

"Fuck you, Mac. You ain't that much taller..."

The black SUV clipped their silver two thousand model Lexus. The teens screamed, Tundra gained control of the car and floored it. The car sped forward, but the black SUV kept pace. Mac looked out the back to see a second SUV joining the chase.

"There's more!" He shouted.

The black SUV slammed into the side of the car. The Lexus slid, Tundra regained control and slammed the Lexus back into the SUV. Sparks flew between the two automobiles, reflected in the slick roads. The second SUV crept up on the Lexus' rear and nudged the car. Tundra gripped the steering wheel.

"Come on!" Cassie urged.

"I'm moving!" Countered Tundra.

She glanced down at the speedometer. It read fifty five. She steered away from the SUV to her left, her foot heavy on top of the pedal. The car responded, pulling away from the aggressive SUVs. Sirens reached their ears. The boys looked out the window to see red and blue lights pulling up to the chase.

"We got help coming!" Timber shouted.

A flash emanated from the rear SUV.

"Shit! Duck!" Mac ordered.

Timber ducked as a bullet smashed through the rear window and struck the headrest on the driver side. Torn fabric showered Tundra's hair.

Bullets slammed into the rear end of the car.

"Tundra!" Timber yelled.

"I'm OK," Tundra called back. "Fuck!"

Ahead of them was a busy intersection just outside the only shopping center in town. The early evening traffic meant every lane was filled. Tundra scanned the area for a side street or any way to circumvent the oncoming calamity.

"Oh shit," Cassie exclaimed. "What do we do?"

"No choice!"

The rear tired suddenly exploded. The car swerved and Tundra struggled to control the wayward vehicle. The SUVs gained ground. The rim hit the asphalt. The high pitched whine of metal on asphalt drowned out the nearing police sirens. Tundra directed the hobbled car across the front of the SUVs and into oncoming traffic.

"What the fuck are they doing?!" Banner shouted from the passenger seat of Phillip's Ford Taurus.

"They're getting desperate," Phillip observed. "And your wife is going to be pissed."

They watched the sparks fly from the damaged Lexus as it dodged oncoming traffic with surprising accuracy. Banner grabbed the radio, and eyeballed the squad cars around him.

"Unit oh five, Unit one-one," he called out.

"Oh five here."

"Unit one-one," screeched through the radio. Both men sounded equally excited and scared.

"Both of you take the closet SUV, and PIT the fuckers. We'll take the lead SUV out."

"Copy."

"Copy, out."

He watched the two cars approach the vehicle. Oh five pulled up beside the truck, preparing to initiate the P.I.T maneuver. The truck's window rolled down and rapid gunfire erupted. The car's windshield shattered under the onslaught. The cabin splattered with blood. The car rolled to the side, out of the show.

The eleven car rammed the rear of the truck. The officer in the passenger seat fired his gun out the side window. Banner grabbed the radio once more.

"Oh five is down, oh seven and two seven, back up one-one," He ordered.

The cars rushed into action as the eleven car struggled to control the truck. The units surrounded the vehicle pouring bullets into the truck. Eleven front wheels were aligned with the SUV's rear wheels. Bullets riddled the hood of their squad car. The car nudged the SUV. The truck's rear tires skid and the one-one car steered into the SUV. The SUV spun out and the one-one car engine died as both vehicles were swarmed by back up. Banner and Phillip continued after the battered Lexus and its pursuing SUV.

"One down," Banner announced. "Now let's get these kids before they hit that intersection."

"Not possible," Phillip pointed out.

"No," he said breathlessly, his heart jumped in his chest.

Banner could make out the sparks flying from the Lexus in the distance. They were just seconds away from causing the second massive car accident of the day.

"Not a good idea!" Tundra shouted.

"Stop!" Cassie pleaded.

"This is it!" Mac hollered.

Tundra slammed her fist on the horn. The car horn blared and they screamed as they drove into the thick traffic. Tundra jerked the wheel to the right, with the oncoming traffic, tires and metal sliding across the slick road.

The side of the silver Lexus smashed into a red Hyundai. The larger Lexus forced the small Elantra into the next lane. Metal screeched and snapped all around them. The black SUV pinned a green Ford truck between them and the Lexus. A four door Accord plowed into the side of the SUV. Several cars rear ended the pile up. Momentum carried the Hyundai and Lexus into oncoming traffic. A maroon Lincoln car hit the Hyundai head on sending it several feet back. Cars swerved around the incident while others stopped in the middle of the intersection. For a moment there was only the wail of police sirens.

Tundra opened her eyes. She pushed the airbag out of her face and scanned her surroundings. Lights reflected off the bent and torn metals.

Her vision was colorful and bright, and it took her a moment to remember the sun had set recently. A moan alerted her. "Cassie," she grabbed her sister's arm.

"I'm alive," she answered, a hand on her head. She grabbed the airbag and ripped it from the dashboard.

"Timber? Mac?"

"Fine," Mac responded, as he brushed shards of shattered glass off his shirt.

"OK, somehow," Timber said softly.

All around cries of pain and shock filled the air around them. Tundra's body ached from being tossed around in her seat, but the seat belt had kept her safe from major harm.

"The safety rating on this thing must be amazing," she remarked.

"We have to get out of here," Timber stated.

"Yes," Tundra agreed.

The car's engine continued to run despite the hammering it had taken. She put her foot on the gas and the car inched forward. Tangled metal between the Ford truck and Lexus whined, the tires spun uselessly against the slick road. Smell of gas, smoke and burnt rubber filled the car's cabin.

"Come on," Cassie urged.

"I'm trying," Tundra turned the steering wheel away from the truck, but the metal held tight.

A man stepped out of the car ahead of them. He stumbled, his eyes wide and glassy, blood seeped from his forehead. A pop rung out and a geyser of blood erupted from his chest. His body fell to the asphalt. Bystanders and those able to move screamed and rushed from their cars. Another shot fired and hot thick liquid hit Cassie's back.

"Oh my God," Mac screamed.

Cassie felt no pain and looked out the passenger window. The driver's head, in the truck pinned against the Lexus, was gone, the remnants all over her back and hair. More shots followed peppering the green truck and hood of the Lexus.

Tundra screamed and slammed her foot on the gas. She pulled at the steering wheel, tires spun, smoke rose. The gunfire was relentless as a new crack of sidearm, shotguns and rifles joined the firefight.

She shifted the car into reverse and slammed on the gas. Metal popped and creaked. She shifted the car back into drive, aimed the wheels for the gap in front of them and slammed her foot on the gas once more. The sedan hobbled away from the truck to cheers from its passengers.

"Stop the car!" Banner ordered Phillip.

Phillip slammed on the brakes, the car skidding to a stop. Ahead of them, surrounded by damaged cars, the men inside the SUV rolled their windows down.

"Get out!" Banner pushed his car door open.

Bullets struck the hood of the car and shattered the windshield. Both detectives threw themselves from the car. Their seats erupted, torn apart, under the onslaught. Phillip crawled to the back of the car.

A squad car screeched to a halt beside Banner. He pulled open the driver's door. "Out," he dragged the man out the car, "and stay down!" Banner stuck his head into the car, the windshield shattered, and showered him with shards of glass. He kept his head below the steering wheel and grabbed the gear shift with his right hand. His left pressed against the brake and he shifted the car into drive.

The vehicle rolled forward under the barrage of bullets. Banner struggled to keep his head down and himself in the automobile. His legs dragged against the asphalt, the driver's door pinned against him. The thump of bullets against metal resonated around him. He gripped the steering wheel and guided the car across the front of Phillip's Taurus. A bullet struck the seat just inches from his shoulder. Fabric exploded in his face and he yelled. He ducked under the steering wheel and punched the brake pedal. Reaching up, he put the car in park and dipped out.

"What the fuck was that?" Phillip ran up on Banner as he shut the door to the bullet ridden police cruiser.

Banner sucked in gulps of air, he shook his head at his luck, and reached for his gun. "Horseshoe," he shouted over the roar of gunfire.

Phillip looked around, and saw they were covered on three sides by cars. "What you just did was fucking crazy," he stated, pulling his own gun out.

"But necessary," Banner waved more officers into their makeshift shelter. "Get over here and put fire down on them."

Banner looked over the cruiser and watched one of the heavily armed men take aim at them. Banner exhaled slowly and fired, the man slammed against the SUV. His bullet had struck the man's exposed throat. The other officers found it difficult to strike down the mercenaries. They were clad in heavy body armor and moved with the precision of highly trained black operatives. A small team of three hopped out the SUV. Using the cars as cover they flanked the small-town cops and overpowered their left with heavy fire. Banner dipped behind the cruiser to reload his glock.

"I got one of them," he called out.

"Who the fuck are you?" Phil yelled over the noise.

"Get our left!" Banner shouted to the officers around him.

Banner rose back up in time to see the small team fall back to the SUV. Inside, the engine roared and the vehicle turned away from them. Banner fired several shots at the fleeing truck.

"They're moving."

"No shit," Phil snapped at his partner and got back in the driver's seat.

The engine still running.

"The kids must've gotten loose."

"Good for them," Phillip put the car in drive and nudge the disable police car out of the way.

Banner got back on the radio asking for back up, and leaving the rest to handle the mess.

"This fucking car is getting us nowhere," Timber spoke into Tundra's ear.

The Lexus' engine groaned and popped in protest. The exposed rim shrieked against asphalt. They all rocked and bounced in the unbalanced vehicle.

"They're gaining," Mac announced.

"Where you want me to stop?"

"Anywhere," Timber stated. "They can't catch us on foot, no one can."

"News flash, Timber, we're not faster than a speeding bullet."

Timber ripped fabric from the shot up headrest. "Neither is this piece of shit," he showed her the fabric in his hands. "And we'd have more room to maneuver than in here."

"Fine!"

She searched their dark surroundings, but found only farmland and trees.

She checked the rearview mirror. The SUV sped up on their rear end. She pulled off the road into the grass, the car bounced on the new surface till she stopped the vehicle.

"Out!" She ordered.

The doors swung open. They leapt out and were greeted by bullets zipping by through the air. They ducked and ran off into the night. The SUV pulled to a stop behind the car and six men stepped out, armed to the teeth. They slipped their night vision goggles on.

Timber led his siblings into a small grove of trees. They laid flat in the wet muddy grass, breathing heavily not from exhaustion, but excitement.

Their hearts raced, muscles flexed with a rush of blood flowing throughout their bodies. Timberland felt himself smile. The energy he felt, built on adrenaline and fear, mixed into a euphoric feeling.

Tundra watched the tight cluster of men creep towards them. Their rifles swept their field of vision from left to right in search of a target. Her fingers dug into the earth in anticipation. Their smell filled her senses, she could sense their mood, hear their quickening heartbeats and the soft wails of police sirens in the distance. The group walked into the cluster of trees.

"Now," Timberland shouted.

Tundra sprung to her feet. She covered the ground between her and the closest armed man in one lengthy jump. She landed on his back with a primal yell. They rolled on the ground, and he struggled to get her off, but she had an arm around his neck locked in a vise grip. Tundra got her knees under her and tightened her grip around his neck.

"Why are you trying to kill us?" She demanded.

The man groaned in pain and swung a fist at her. She shook his body like a ragdoll and tightened her grip.

"Tell me!"

"Fuck you," he spat out between gasps for air.

"Don't make me kill you," she threatened.

"You're a monster," he growled. "They should've never made you."

"I'm a monster? You killed my mother!"

She squeezed harder. The man's arm shot upward. Light reflected off the steel blade in his hand. Tundra's free hand caught the man's wrist. He strained against her grip to no avail.

"Make me a monster," she whispered into the man's ear.

He gurgled and wheezed. His face darkened and eyes bulged out. Mouth agape, tongue dangling, his leg kicked and dug into the ground for leverage. Tundra gave one final squeeze, heard the windpipe pop under the pressure. The man's body went into convulsions. She stepped back and watched the man claw at his throat till he went still. She stared at the lifeless body for a moment.

"Fucker," she spat out.

Tundra turned to see if her siblings were okay. She saw Timber going through the pockets of one of the three bodies around him. Mac drugged a body behind him.

"You could've saved one of them for me," he commented.

Timber shrugged his shoulders, and pulled a radio out of one of the men's pockets.

"You should've been faster, then."

Tundra drugged her victim over by his leg and set him down. Sirens roared louder as they neared the scene of the abandoned automobiles.

"I didn't even hear them get a shot off," she commented.

"We should take weapons," Timber began unzipping the dead man's vest. The corpse's head rolled loosely on its broken neck. "They'll send more."

Mac lifted a rifle off his kill. He looked the lightweight metallic weapon up and down. He casually waved it about while investigating. Pressing a button on the right side, the magazine clip slid out and flopped in the wet grass.

"That's what that does," he said while retrieving the fallen clip.

"Man, watch where you are waving that thing," Timber warned and slipped an armored vest on.

Mac turned away from his siblings, nodding his head. Timber opened and closed various Velcro pockets on the vest. Tundra began to remove the vest from the man she had killed. Timber noticed a knife in one of his pockets. He pulled it out and stared at the serrated blade.

"Did we get everybody?" Tundra asked, as she too slipped a vest on.

"Not everybody," Cassie called out to her siblings.

They walked over to find Cassie watching a man crawl away from her. He groaned in pain, slowly pulling himself forward in the muddy wet grass. His legs dragged behind him, useless.

"What the fuck you do?" Tundra asked, curiosity in her voice.

"Threw him into a tree. Guess I snapped his spine," she answered.

They stared at the wounded man with mixed emotions. Their apathy to his suffering surprised them. In under twelve hours they'd left a trail of bodies in their attempts to survive. Why had it been so easy for them to take a life?

Timber shook his head, could feel the unease in the air. "We need answers," he said.

The group stalked the desperate man like a pack of predators surrounding a wounded buffalo. The man noticed the feet surrounding him and stopped. His body slumped into the wet grass. Timber flipped the man onto his back, grabbed him by his neck and propped him against a tree.

"Why are you doing this?" Timber growled at him.

The man took a moment to adjust to the four pairs of flickering eyes before him.

"The rumors are true," he muttered under his breath.

"What rumors?"

The man finally looked Timber in the eyes.

"Fuck you," he said.

Timber slapped the man hard across the face and squeezed his hand around the man's neck. The man gasped for air and feebly swung at Timber's head. Timber easily deflected the man's attempt and slammed him against the tree. His hands went up to pry Timber's hand from his neck. The boy's fingers were like unrelenting steel coils. Timber loosened his grip slightly.

"Talk, motherfucker," Timber yelled.

The man coughed and spit blood from his mouth. He stared back at Timber, his lips sealed.

"Just fucking smash his head into the tree," Mac barked.

"Naw, that's too easy for him. I want my fucking answers."

"These guys are trained not to talk, Timber," Cassie pointed out.

Timber retrieved the knife from its sheath. He made sure the man could see it in the dark. Rain popped against the tree canopy above. Cold water hung in the air, casting a light mist above the grass.

"You hear those sirens?" Timber asked. "We led you fuckers almost a mile out from the cars. It'll be a few minutes before they get to you."

Timber held the knife's handle to his palm with his thumb. He used his fingers to grip the man's thigh. He shut his eyes and concentrated, feeling the pulse, then opened his eyes.

"I want to know what you know."

The man stared at Timber. A minute passed with not a word. Tundra looked over her shoulder at the red and blue lights flashing in the distance. Timber sighed and plunged the knife into the man's thigh. The man's eyes opened wide and his hand grabbed Timber's forearm.

"Whoa, don't move it," Timber warned. "I nicked your artery, man. I

112

told you I want to know. You tell me what I want to hear, we'll get the cops here. They'll save your life. If not, I'll remove this blade and your minutes of survival turn into seconds."

"Bill Saunders, ex-Seal." Bill spurted out, his voice high with fear. "I work for Brighton Services. We were hired by Lane Industries to retrieve missing property."

"Property?" Tundra asked.

"According to them, you belong to them."

"Why?" Timberland asked.

"I don't know, I'm just a hired gun."

"What of the rumors?"

"Rumors?" Bill's face became pale and his head rolled back, face wet from rain.

Timber shook the man. "Focus, you said something about rumors."

"Rumors..." He nodded his head. "Something about an experiment gone wrong."

Timber tightened his grip on the handle. "Where?"

"Here... No wait, not here," Bill glanced upwards.

"Columbus?" Tundra asked.

"Yes," he leaned his head back against the tree. "They thought you were dead after some engagement. I wasn't there. That's all I know." Timber removed the blade from the man's thigh.

"What? I told you everything I know!" He pleaded.

"You killed my mother," Timber's voice cracked. His hands shook as he stepped back.

"Get me help," Bill put a hand over the wound. Blood pumped profusely out drowning his hands. "Don't let me die, not like this."

They watched the pleading man's life drain from him. His body slumped over, breathing labored, skin pale. His chest slowed and then stopped.

"I guess this confirms our dreams," Tundra noted shattering the silence.

"No more speculations."

"Let's get out of here," Timber cleared his throat. "Strip the bodies of everything useful, and we'll disappear before the cops get here."

"How did we get to this?" Cassie asked.

The others ignored her question. Each of them dealt with the sudden turn their lives had taken. Bewildered and frightened they stripped the dead bodies of weapons and ammo.

8:10PM

Banner shifted through documents and garbage retrieved from the glove box of his totaled Lexus. He balanced on one buttock in the passenger seat to avoid the shattered glass. Outside his car, officers scoured the wreckage for evidence. A team hit the field just moments ago in search of the missing teens.

Banner sat back, staring out the shattered remnants of his windshield. Smoke rose up from the caved in hood. Emergency lights danced along the wet aluminum. Smells of spent rubber and gas filled the foggy night air.

"If you need a bodyguard when you tell the wife about this, don't think of me," Phil stepped up beside his shell shocked friend.

Banner stuffed the documents he deemed important into his coat pocket and stepped out of the car. Glass rolled off his coat and fell onto the ground. He locked eyes with his partner, ignored the man's cocky grin.

"Oh you don't have to worry," Banner assured him. "She'll just be glad we don't have to trade her car in for a minivan."

"Don't these cars come with an airbag?" Phillip asked, his head inside the vehicle.

"Yeah, I guess they ripped them out."

Banner made his way to the truck that had pursued the frightened kids.

Phillip hurried to catch up. Flares cast everything in a reddish glow.

"These kids are a beast," Phillip commented.

"What do we have over here?" Banner asked the officers surrounding the black SUV.

"Nothing," an officer wearing bright blue gloves responded from the driver's seat. "This car is custom made."

"Custom?" Phillip asked.

"No VIN number, no make or model insignia. Armored windows and siding."

A drill whined behind the officer.

"We found a high powered satellite communication radio under the dash. It's heavily encrypted and they appeared to lock it down before they left the vehicle. We're removing it to see if we can crack it."

"Make it quick," Banner ordered. "We're dealing with some heavy duty shit. Can't take our time."

"Of course," the officer responded.

Banner stepped away from the truck only to cross paths with his boss. Sheriff Winslow, a former Vietnam vet with broad shoulders on a slim fit frame and a thick silver mustache to go with his silver hair, approached his top detectives. His brown gallon hat and matching uniform gave him the look of a gunslinger.

"Dammit Banner, how you let four kids run out of a police station?" He spoke with a soft Kentucky drawl.

"Sir, I wasn't given much of a choice," Banner stated.

"How so? Didn't take a former city cop like you to be such a pushover," He eyed Banner for a reaction. "Let me give you a lesson. They're kids, you give the orders, and they obey."

"You know my record," Banner stated calmly. "I'm no pushover. These kids are not your average kids."

Winslow crossed his arms, a sneer on his face. "How do you expect

116

to be a good father if you can't keep a bunch of unruly kids in a building full of cops?"

"Sir, I..." Banner's brow furrowed and he took a step back from the Sheriff. His biceps twitched as he held back to urge to physically react.

"I, Banner, have just got back from cleaning up their mess on Seventy and I come into my town to see this. We got three towns and three hospitals dealing with that shit earlier and now this? Civilians are dead and I have two cops in critical condition, Parker and Ellis, and Ellis doesn't look like he's going to make it. You want to tell his family he's not coming home because you couldn't keep a few kids in check?"

Winslow stepped closer to the detective. Banner stood a good half a foot taller than his boss. Winslow's pale white skin transformed to crimson, his rage building.

"Winslow, you do not put Ellis on me," Banner stood his ground. "I've done all I can to keep those kids in that building. Whoever is chasing them is at fault."

Both men's voices rose and caught the attention of everyone around them. Phillip stepped between the two. He directed Banner away from their boss.

"I need this to be over, Banner," Winslow shouted. "We can't afford any more bloodshed!"

Banner slapped Phillip's hand away from him once they were a safe distance from the enraged sheriff. His hands balled into tight fists, he sucked in gulps of air to calm himself.

"The fuck is that guy's problem?" Banner asked. "Putting Ellis on me. Putting all of this on me. Fuck him."

"Whoa, calm down man. You know Ellis is his friend's son."

"Oh, so blame all this shit on the outsider? Is that what you people do here, Phil?"

"We know this isn't your fault," Phillip put a hand on his friend's shoulder. "He just needed to vent."

"Yeah, well still fuck him." Banner's radio crackled.

"We found... something," the voice appeared to struggle with his words.

Banner retrieved his radio from his belt buckle. "Is it the kids? What is it?" He asked.

"It's a fucking mess, sir."

Banner and Phillip looked to each other, concern etched on their faces. Together they dashed off into the field, a team of officers behind them. A man guided them with a wave of his flashlight. He stood in front of a clump of trees.

Banner approached the man. He recognized him as Anferny Waites, an officer with the department for ten years. Waites lowered his flashlight. His eyes opened wide, he walked past the detective and back to the road shaking his head. The detectives walked into the cluster of trees towards a group of flashlights. Another officer brushed past him in the darkness.

He could hear the man vomit behind him.

"This can't be good," Phillip said.

They stopped at the pile of bodies. He counted five men in various stages of undress. Their bodies were cold, wet, devoid of color.

"The kids?" Banner asked, waving his flashlight along the ground in search of them.

"Gone," an officer said, his voice soft. "They did this?"

Winslow shoved his way forward and stopped beside Banner. Banner noticed the familiarity in the man's eyes. This wasn't the worst he'd seen.

"Yeah, I think it's safe to say they did this," Banner answered.

"There's another one over here," a voice called out in the darkness.

They followed the voice to find an officer standing over a body against a tree. The grass around the man was dark and matted with blood, his skin blue and wet, appearing like plastic.

"They bled him out," the officer pointed out.

Banner stepped closer to the dead mercenary, stared into the man's glassy eye. "Put the highway patrol on alert," he ordered, stepping away from the body. "I want a statewide APB out on these kids. They're scared and heavily armed. Tell them to approach with caution, and these kids are not to be harmed! You understand?"

"Yes sir," the group called out.

"Get these bodies bagged, search them for any identification. I doubt you'll find any, but be thorough anyway."

The group dispersed to their duties. Banner looked to the old man and strutted over to him. Winslow's eyes locked on the dead man.

"Still think these are just kids?"

8:25PM

"They look disturbed," Timber pointed out.

He blinked several times to bring his sight out of, as they called it, binocular vision. He rubbed his eyes and turned to face his siblings.

Tundra and Cassie were huddled together, Mac with his back to them. Cassie's face was an image of worry in the misty night. Tundra's sympathetic arm draped around her sister's shoulder.

"You should be too," Cassie remarked.

Timber stepped back into the shrubs where they were hiding. At least a mile of open field separated them from the officers in the clump of trees.

"How's it going with the radio?" Timber asked Mac, who fiddled with the phone they had pulled off one of the bodies.

"I don't know," the anxious boy called back over his shoulder. "There's like a security lock on this or something."

Timber moved next to his brother. He reached for the phone, but Mac pulled away. Timber punched his shoulder. Mac elbowed him in return.

"I can't stop my hands from shaking," Cassie told Tundra.

"Me neither," Tundra related. "Too much adrenaline right now."

"I don't think that's it," she shook her head. "I'm freaking out, I have some innocent guy's blood on my back!"

"We are going to have to get you a new shirt."

"Whoa," Mac exclaimed as the phone rang in his hand.

He hit the answer button and held the phone out.

"Echo, check in," a male voice called out from the thick brick shaped black phone.

"Echo is gone," Mac informed the voice.

"Who is this? Where is Echo team? How did you get this phone?" The voice sounded alarmed.

"They tried to kill us and failed," Mac stated. The voice didn't immediately respond. "That should answer all of your questions, right? I got some of my own. You the one that started this shit? If not, I'm not going to waste my breath on you."

"Hold," the discouraged voice responded.

The line went dead. Mac looked at his siblings. They wore a mix of excitement and fear on their faces. He chuckled to himself. "We about to get somewhere finally," he pointed out.

"That's what I'm afraid of," Tundra said.

"Why?"

"People are trying to kill us. This isn't a game," Cassie cried out.

"I know," Mac shrugged.

"Maybe, we should disappear," Tundra suggested.

"And forget what happened today?" Mac stood up. "Forget Mom?"

"No, Mac," Tundra threw her arms up and down. "This doesn't end don't you get that?"

"Mac," Timber put a hand on his brother's shoulder. "Mercenaries are being hired to capture us. Nothing good comes when that phone rings again, but we are not disappearing. They started this... Only we can finish this."

8:30PM
SOMEWHERE OVER INDIANA

Nathaniel Porter sat at a small table in the rear fuselage of a prototype Gulfstream jet. He cradled a cup of coffee in his hands. He stared into the dark liquid. In hours he would be sharing a room with his greatest achievement. His heart pounded with anticipation. Tonight he would regain a family.

Leg nervously jiggling, he looked for something to calm his nerves. Across the circular marble table sat Pam. Porter eyed her firm body. The young assistant's obsession with physical fitness was his top reason for hiring her. It had paid off tenfold for him as flashes of their affair crossed his mind. He watched her pick up the phone. He looked around the cabin and wondered if they could squeeze in a quick session before they landed in Columbus.

"Porter," her voice cut through his thoughts.

"Huh?" He asked, bringing his focus back to her.

"It's them," she held the phone out for him.

"Them who?" He took the phone from her and pressed the receiver to his ear.

"Them," she emphasized.

Their eyes locked on each other. The phone shook against his ear. He felt foolish, like a fourteen year old receiving a call from his crush. He cleared his throat.

"Who is this?" A low voice boomed in his ear.

He immediately recognized the speaker. The boy's voice was raspy and low since he uttered his first words. He ran through his mental notes to retrieve the name the woman, Jamila, hid him under.

"Mackenzie," Porter's heart leaped into his throat, choking off his words. "I'm Nathaniel Porter, I can't believe... You sound so grown up."

8:31PM
EVANSVILLE, OH

Mac looked at his siblings. They expressed the bewilderment he felt. They didn't know what to expect, but an emotional response was the last thing.

"Are you the man in charge?" The only question that popped into the young man's mind.

"Yes," Porter answered.

"Why are you doing this?"

Porter sighed. The phone was silent for a long moment. Mac was about to ask if he was still there when Porter suddenly spoke.

"You're mines," he stated. "I spent decades of my life to bring you into this world. There's nothing I wouldn't do to have you back in my life."

"Get us back?" Tundra muttered, unconvinced.

"You killed our mother. You tried to kill us," Cassie cried out.

"I gave no such order to you," he cleared his throat. "And she was never your mother."

"Fuck you," Mac snapped, his fingers squeezed the phone. The plastic cracked under the pressure. "She gave us everything, we were strangers. She didn't have to, but she did."

"Fuck me?" They heard a thump on the other end as Porter slammed his hand against the marble table. "I gave you life. You think you've lost someone? I lost everyone I loved that night you were taken from me. I will scorch the earth to get just a piece of my family back together."

"I guess it's only fitting since you gave us life," Mac looked back at his siblings. Their faces twisted in anger. "That we end yours."

"Poetic," Porter chuckled. "Come home. You remember where home is?"

"You killed our home," Tundra shouted over Mac's shoulder.

"We can rebuild our home," Porter said.

"We'll use your dead body as foundation," Mac growled.

"Home," Porter said softly. "You remember?"

"We'll see you."

The connection ended. Mac flung the phone into the night. He let out a frustrated yell.

"That's it," Mac glared at Timber. "The fucker signed his death warrant."

"We go now," Timber added.

"How?" Caspian asked.

"We run."

"Almost sixty miles, Timber," Tundra pointed out.

"I know what the distance is."

"We can do that easy," Mac chimed in. "We've never been tired running."

"Yeah running circles around our little town isn't the same as running across a state," Tundra stated.

"Well, I'm not getting in another car," Mac pointed out. "Especially if you're driving."

"We're doing this," Timber ordered.

"And then what?" Cassie stepped back into the group, her hands up and her face flushed. "We haven't thought a single action through."

"Kind of hard to stop and think when you wake up chained to the floor," Timber countered.

"She's right," Tundra said. She moved to stand at her sister's side. "I haven't made the best of decisions for us."

Timber took in his sisters' mood and stepped back. Mac crossed his arms and shook his head with impatience.

"Look at us," Cassie grabbed her dirty top. "Wet, dirty, and covered in someone else's blood."

"Not our fault," Mac countered.

"It's not, but the blood on me isn't just from those chasing us. A man's head was blown off right beside us."

"I know, I saw, but we didn't pull that trigger."

"How did he end up in front of that gun? We have to be smart."

"Whatever we're in," a calmer Timber spoke up. "We need to keep it between us and them."

"That's what I'm saying."

"Our actions," he continued, "have led to the suffering of others. Yes we didn't start this, but we clearly have the power to keep this from affecting others."

"Collateral damage," Tundra referenced.

"Horrible movie," Mac mentioned. Timber shoved him.

"So we can't have another chase end in a pile up where we walk out unscathed while innocents suffer around us," Cassie drove home the point.

"What do we do about Columbus then?" Mac asked.

"It's clearly a trap, but we have little choice. To end this we need to get to the man who started it."

"Yeah, and from the sounds of him that dude is fucked in the head," Tundra said. "He's not going to stop."

"We run to Columbus," Timber announced. "We get ourselves fed and rested. And then, from a safe distance, we scope out the building from our dreams."

"Ugh, I hate where this is heading," Cassie groaned and looked to the east.

The rest faced eastward and walked towards Columbus. They fiddled with the gun straps till they had the automatic rifles strapped tightly across their backs. Weapons secured, they picked up their speed and began their long trek.

9:50 PM

Banner and Phillip watched the last body being loaded into the back of an ambulance. The rain finally stopped and a cold front moved in, thickening the fog around them. The search teams returned with no sign of the kids. Available cruisers from neighboring towns scoured the roads around the crash site.

Winslow approached his two detectives with a cell phone pressed against his ear. He said a couple of inaudible words before flipping the phone closed. The sight of his boss' phone reminded Banner of his own phone still sitting on his desk in his office. He wondered how many missed calls and angry voice messages awaited him.

"I need you two back at the station," Winslow's voice cut into Banner's thoughts.

"What for?" Phillip asked. "The kids are still out there."

"I get that," Winslow acknowledged with a nod. "There's not much for you to do here. Besides, the FBI are sending their people in to assist."

"FBI?" Banner's eyebrows rose. "Our little town warrants their presence?"

"You know kidnappings fall under their jurisdiction."

"Oh, I'm aware. I'm just not sure if we are protecting the kids from their captors or the captors from the kids."

Banner dropped the evidence bag, filled with the personal items retrieved from his totaled car, onto his desk. He sat in his chair and immediately looked for his cell phone. He found it buried under fast food wrapping paper. He flipped the small gunmetal colored phone open. The display read twenty missed calls, with an equal amount of voice message recordings and double the text messages awaiting him.

He didn't bother to check the messages and dialed Sondra Banner's number. She picked up on the first ring. Her tone far from pleasant.

"Why haven't answered your phone?" She snapped, her words hurried.

"Hey honey, I'm fine," he answered.

"Then why didn't you answer?" He began to respond, but she continued. "I've been watching the news and they just keep showing smashed cars. I called Emily; she said she last saw you just before the second pile up. They're saying people were shot!"

"Yes, there was..."

"I had to play phone tag with the other wives."

"I'm sorry, I had..."

"They didn't know anything. Everyone's telling me you're okay, but you're not answering me!"

"The phone was on my desk all this time," Banner explained. He took slight pleasure in her panic for his safety.

"I thought you left the Columbus PD to get away from the violence," Sondra stammered. "Tired of death following you."

"I guess death found me," Banner sighed. "Arrived in the form of four little kids."

"Jamila's kids?" Sondra's voice dropped to a concerned whisper. "How are they?"

"I wish I could tell you," he stared at the empty bags and cups in front of him. "This day gets weirder with every hour that passes."

"Well I have faith you'll find them sweetie," he could hear his wife get choked up. "She was an incredible mother to those kids. She did not deserve this."

"You've spent some time with Jamila right?"

"Only seen her around the school a couple times," she remembered.

"Only small talk. I didn't really know her well."

"She tell you anything about her kids?"

"Well of course, she loved those kids," she paused for a moment. "What are you trying to get at? You think they did this? Sure they were little terrors, but they love her more than anything."

"No, I'm not saying that," he assured her. "Just the things I've seen... I just need to know how she ended up with them. I can't really find a record on them. She lived in Columbus before she moved here, right?"

"Right, after her divorce," Sondra recollected. "She told me that much. Small town life for her and her new family."

"Nothing else? No reason behind going from divorced to having four kids."

"Just that the Lord took her gift to give life away and someone saw fit to give her an opportunity."

"An opportunity? And who is someone?"

"To be a mother and I figured she meant the kids. Why are you grilling me? I told you I only spoke with her briefly."

"I'm sorry."

"When are you coming home? We miss you."

Banner smiled. He figured she was looking at her pregnant belly. Her hands caressing it. He frowned at the work ahead of him.

"Not tonight," he could hear her sulk. "The FBI will be here in the morning and Phil and I have to get this mess sorted to fill them in."

"Okay, but can you do us a favor?"

"Anything, what is it?"

"Keep your fucking phone on you."

Banner chuckled at her sudden change.

"Yes ma'am. I love you."

"We love you too."

11:45 PM

Banner dropped the printed out articles on his desk. He leaned back in his seat and let out a yawn. The remnants of a lasagna dinner, courtesy of Phillip's wife Penelope, with peas and spinach as sides sat next to the keyboard in a Tupperware case.

The bags and paper from Wendy's still cluttered his desk. Phillip sat in one of the two chairs. The box of medical records sat next to him on the floor. His feet were up, resting on the edge of Banner's desk. He used his lap to hold the folders, a small medical dictionary, and a notepad.

Sarah walked into his office with a short stack of papers in her hands. She reached over Phillip's feet and placed them on top of the articles. Banner scooped up the papers and leaned back in his seat.

"That's all I can get from the Springfield Fire Department on the fire that killed Doctor Suggs," she announced.

She shook Phillip's legs by his ankles. He dropped his legs back to the floor and let her by. Then returned his feet to their original position.

Sarah flopped down into the vacant chair.

"Thank you," Banner said, flipping through the pages. "You with us for the night?'

"Yep."

"You know Maurice can handle all this," Phillip pointed out, referring to the night shift clerk. He wrote out something on his pad.

"Maurice has the worried civilians and press to deal with," she countered.

"Any word on Ellis?" Banner asked.

"Out of surgery, took quite a few bullets but they were able to get them all out. Now we wait to see if he can make it through the next twenty four hours. Doctor says if he gets through that, his chances of recovery increase dramatically. They upgraded Parker to stable."

"That's good," Phillip said.

"So you think these medical records will help you figure out who is after these kids?" Sarah asked.

"Someone is after these kids, and I can tell you it is not for money," Banner placed the arson report down. "These kids are special."

"He's not lying," Phillip dropped his legs back to the floor and sat up. He held up his notepad and returned the folder back to the box beside him. "According to these files, when you put it all together, these kids are super."

"Yeah the pile of bodies they left us kind of told me that already," Banner teased.

"No, I mean no human is built like this. It's like someone went into their genetics, and they triggered certain mutations, or manipulated their DNA, to get the results they desired."

"Is that even possible?" Sarah asked.

"I'm no doctor and I'm just putting together what I can with an outdated medical dictionary, but that's what these files are telling me."

"Well, Jamila always said it was like they appeared out of thin air."

"Thin air?" Banner inquired.

"Well, yeah," Sarah scooted her seat closer to Banner's desk happy she was able to contribute. "She told me how they were found on the highway. It was sometime in the late eighties or early nineties. I can't really remember exactly."

"Kids found on the highway? They must've been really young," Banner tapped his finger against the desk, his mind mulling over an old memory.

"Yeah, actually on an exit ramp really close to a busy intersection."

"Ha," Banner struck his desk with an open hand, a smile on his face. "I remember that. Shit, I think it was off of the Alum Creek exit."

"She never said which," Sarah clarified. "But if that's a busy intersection. That could be them."

"Oh it can get pretty busy."

"You were an officer then?" Phillip asked.

"Yeah, I was only in for a couple years at that point. I didn't work that side of town. An old partner of mines told me about some kids he found on an exit ramp around that time."

Banner picked up his desk phone and dialed a number. "Maybe he can answer some questions for us," the other end rang. "He might know how Jamila is involved in this. If these are the same kids."

"Hello?" The familiar voice called out.

"Cliff, it's Banner."

11:50PM
COLUMBUS, OH

Clifford Turner slid out of his green Ford Taurus into a light drizzle. He flipped the collar of his tan trench coat to protect his small cell phone and keep the water off the back of his neck. He didn't bother to close the front of the coat. The rain assaulted the part of his shirt protruding from the protection of his coat, pushed out by his keg sized belly.

"Banner," he smiled. "It's been a couple months since I've heard from you. How are you?"

He walked into a Steak n Shake restaurant. He reached up to shake the water loose from his cropped brown hair.

"I'm in a bind," Banner answered.

Clifford took a seat on a stool at the counter. The stool creaked in protest. The waitress recognized him and mouthed if he wanted the usual.

He nodded. "What kind of bind?" He asked.

"You got the APB we put out on four missing kids?"

"Yeah, I thought that came from your little town. What is going on down there?"

"More than I ever expected."

The waitress placed a cup of coffee in front of the detective. It was made just the way he liked it. He took a sip.

"The small town life not as quiet as you expected huh?"

"Hey, we can all use a little noise in our lives at some time."

"So what you need from me?" Turner put down the cup.

"You remember those kids you found near Alum Creek Drive, back in nineteen-ninety."

"Ninety?" Cliff sipped from his coffee. "Four kids? One with white hair and they all had creepy little eyes. I remember, why?"

"They're the same kids," Banner informed his old friend.

"The same?" Clifford reached into his inside pocket and retrieved his notepad and pen.

"Yeah, and the people after these kids are probably the ones who lost them in the first place," Banner realized the fact as the words left his mouth.

"Okay, what you need from me?" he covered the receiver end of his phone. "To go," he informed the waitress who nodded in return.

"What happened with those kids?" Banner asked.

"Well we gave them to social services," Cliff recalled. "Then some guy from BCI showed up. Told us he needed me and my partner at the time to show him where we found the kids. After we did that he had us pick the kids up and transport them to some Arab woman's house."

Banner caught the earnest expression on Sarah's face. "Do you remember the woman's name? Was it Jamila?"

"No, sorry can't recall. Not even the agent's name either. I'm sure there's record of it somewhere. I'll find out for you."

"Thank you, Clifford."

"No problem."

September 21st, 2002

12AM
EVANSVILLE

Banner hung up the phone. His two co-workers stared back at him. He smiled and grabbed the Tupperware.

"I think this revelation deserves a bite," he said, stuffing a fork full of cool lasagna into his mouth.

"So you think Jamila is the woman he was speaking of?" Sarah asked.

"Sounds about right," Banner replied after swallowing his food. "We find the BCI Agent, maybe he can shine a light on this. Maybe, he can tell us how Jamila was involved in all of this."

"The kids are cooked up in a lab," Phillip chimed in. "They are lost somehow. An agent arrives after the kids are found and gives them to a recently divorced woman? This hypothesis is a little out there."

"This whole day has been out there. Besides, what else do we have to go on?"

Winslow appeared at doorway. The man looked exhausted, with red eyes and disheveled thin hair. He stared into each person's eyes in the room. "Any leads?" He asked.

"A shaky one at best," Banner answered. He could tell the old man was shaken by something bad.

Winslow nodded. He began to turn away, but stopped and turned back. He cleared his throat.

"Ellis passed away," his voice cracked as the words left his lips.

Banner felt like he been punched in his chest, and sat back in his seat. Phillip dropped his head in his hands as a soft almost inaudible sound escaped Sarah's mouth.

"I'm sorry," Banner said. His eyes stared blankly forward. The orders he gave echoed in his head, along with parting words Cliff gave him years ago.

Winslow grunted and walked away.

SEPTEMBER 2OTH, 2002
11:35 PM
EASTBOUND I-70

Their feet pounded the soft earth. Dirt, grass and water kicked up, covering them in a molasses-like thick mud. Sweat covered them in a reflective shine.

Her eyes deep black pools of sorrow, Tundra led her siblings in single file. The wind battered her, her face soaked in tears and sweat. Her hair flapped behind her like a flag. Wind roaring past her ears created a surreal and deafening effect, isolating her from the ambiance of traffic passing by along I-70 heading east.

Before her, just out of reach, was a vision of her mother. Jamila's warming smile lead them eastward. Tundra's legs pumped harder to reach her. Just maybe, she could wrap her arms around her once more, but her mother continued to smile in the distance. Never closer, the frustration propelled her.

Hours into their run, they felt no need to slow down. Each gulp of air revitalized their every step. Never in their lives had they felt so powerful. Their legs pumped like thoroughbred horses. Adrenaline energized muscles that felt as if they grew stronger with each mile.

Just ahead, cast in moonlight, stood a green traffic sign. It alerted them to the exit for London; only forty miles till they reached Columbus. The sign quickly approached them. Tundra reached up and smacked the sign as she ducked underneath it. The sign reverberated under the blast, the noise breaking through the wind barrier whipping around her head. She heard the sign rattle three more times.

Jamila's smile still awaited her. Tundra madly reached out and stumbled. Mac's hand grabbed the back of her shirt, steadying her. Tundra cried out in protest.

"Be strong," she remembered her mother telling her one night. Every night before bed, mother made sure her kids got quality one-on-one time.

Tundra remembered their talks. She always cherished them above everything else. On many nights Jamila reminded the girl of her role with her siblings, their admiration of her and devotion.

"They believe in you," she told her. "Be strong for them and smart. They will follow you to hell and back."

She didn't feel either trait then, and definitely not now, reaching for a figment of her imagination, running them out of a perfectly safe police station.

"Whether you feel you deserve this or not they chose you," Jamila told her after she questioned herself as she did now.

"But what about Timber? He's smarter and calmer than me. I don't see why he would look up to me," she countered.

She remembered Jamila's patient sigh and her arms wrapping around her. The sweet smell of cinnamon washed over her as her mother pulled her in.

"Timberland is a leader much like you, but he sees what I see in you. You're willing to make a decision and that's all being a leader is. Timber will lead one day, maybe be a manager or owner of his own business, but he has to learn to make a decision. He has to learn that from you."

"And if I make a wrong one?"

Jamila kissed her forehead. Tundra could feel that kiss now, her heart broke.

"Every leader does."

A truck horn blasted through the wind, her memory washed over by the harsh noise. They looked over their left shoulders as a tractor-trailer pulled up beside them. Their eyes reflected his headlights and the moon. They watched the man's head snap back and forth from them to his speedometer. The truck sped up and passed them by.

Annoyed, Tundra looked forward again. There she was, still smiling. Tundra pumped her arms and legs faster, pulled further away from the road.

"Come on," she shouted. "Not much longer to go!"

1:13AM
EVANSVILLE

Banner jumped at the rapping on the doorframe to his office. He caught the pen in his mouth before it fell into his throat, and spat it out. "How could you let me fall asleep with a pen in my mouth?" He asked Phillip.

Phillip sat up, rubbed his eyes and yawned. "That's a question you should ask yourself," he countered. "I was out before you. Besides, Sarah should've saved you."

He looked over at the empty chair beside him.

"Where'd she go?"

Banner pointed behind Phillip. He turned around to see Sarah curled up on the loveseat. Unmoved by the noise her chest rose and dropped rhythmically.

A throat cleared, brought Banner and Phillip's attention back to the door. A short tanned man with thick black hair and wide shoulders stood in the doorway. His wide framed black glasses reflected the fluorescent lights.

"Maurice," Banner scratched his head and stretched his back. "Are you going to answer that?"

"It's just reporters," Maurice looked back at his desk. The phone's rings echoed through the building. "They are intrigued about the current events here."

"What do you have for us?"

"Just got a report in," Maurice said, his voice echoed in the lightly staffed building. "A trucker spotted the kids running along I-70 east."

"Running?" Sarah asked, sitting up. "Are they being chased?"

"No, the trucker reported seeing only them."

"Why are they running?" Phillip asked.

"Well, there's nothing in their file about stealing cars. Safe to say they don't know how to hot-wire one," Banner answered.

"I don't know about that," Maurice countered.

"Why?"

"The report of the sighting was just outside of London."

"London, that's almost thirty miles away right?" Sarah asked.

"Just about," Phillip answered.

"You think they picked up a car, then decided to run after it broke down or ran out of gas?" Banner asked Maurice.

"It's plausible," Maurice pushed his glasses back up the bridge of his nose. "You believe they ran all that way?"

"It's been about five hours since we lost them in the woods..."

"The trucker reported seeing the kids almost two hours ago," Maurice clarified.

"I don't think a group of kids can go from being kidnapped to coming out of a car wreck, and still be well enough to run a marathon afterwards," Phillip interjected.

"Besides," Sarah joined in, slipping back into the chair beside Phillip. "People spend months training for marathons. A fifteen year old can't just jump up and run all that way without crashing."

"Also, the trucker reported seeing them carrying guns," Maurice added.

Banner stood up, retrieved his coat off the back of his chair, and headed towards Maurice. Phillip followed suit, ready to move. Maurice stepped back, allowing Banner passage.

"We're going to have to catch up with them," Banner said, slipping his coat on. "They just answered our question on where they're going."

"No," Winslow said. He looked shabby, his exhaustion and grief visible.

His voice startled them. No one had heard him moving towards Banner's office.

"No?" Banner asked. "We have to get to those kids before they get themselves in trouble."

"I'll alert highway patrol," Winslow grumbled. "After the FBI arrives, you can go get them."

Winslow turned away and disappeared back into his office before the others could cry foul. Banner took his coat off, flung it to the floor beside his desk, and flopped down into his chair.

"Where the fuck are those agents?"

1:45 AM
COLUMBUS, OH

Hunched over, she sucked in gulps of humid air. Her muscles ached and spasm, forcing her whole body to shake. Mac walked by her with his hands on his hips, his head tossed back, looking up at the cloudy night sky. He let out a loud rumble, a groan, to her dismay. She shoved him.

"Be quiet, people are sleeping," she told him, pointing at the house they stood in front of. "Last thing we need is the cops being called on us for disturbing the peace."

"What we need are some fucking medals," Mac countered. He stepped out of Tundra's reach. "What we run, like sixty, eighty miles?"

"Just about," Cassie said with a cough. She busied herself clawing out the mud from her once pristine white hair.

"Shit, a Kenyan should be sucking my dick right now."

"Ew," Cassie shook her head.

"You notice how he didn't specify male or female," Timberland pointed out, and flicked mud at his brother.

"I knew there were questions about you, Mac," Tundra teased.

"Fuck you," Mac shrugged off their comments. "You know I'm all about the titties."

"Do I?" Tundra raised her eyebrows.

"Can you stop talking like that," Cassie pleaded.

"Yeah, yeah," Mac agreed.

He shook his flak jacket and pulled on it to allow air to reach his sweat drenched shirt. Clumps of mud flew off and landed around him. He finally took notice of his shoes. They were caked in mud.

"Aw no, my Kobes," he whined. He sat down on someone's lawn to remove his shoes.

"No," Tundra grabbed Mac's hand and began pulling him back to his feet.

"What the hell are you doing?"

"You can't sit down," she warned. "You sit, you'll never get back up."

"Well damn, we only took three breaks on the way here. I think we can rest right now."

"No, we have to eat. Once we get in the Waffle House you can rest."

"Where is there a Waffle House?"

"Down the street, you dork," Timber jumped in, starving and annoyed at the back and forth.

Mac looked down the street. He could see the yellow squares with black lettering inside, glowing.

"I can eat," he said. "Why didn't we just stop there? Could've saved ourselves some time."

"I'm going to strangle him," Timber announced.

Tundra shoved Mac forward.

"Get moving, we have to find a place to dump these weapons before we go in."

They moved down the street till they reached a fence covered in foliage that separated the business from the residential neighborhood.

Squatting in the shadows, Tundra peered across the nearly empty parking lot. Two walls of the small business were mostly glass giving her full view of the dining area. The place was empty save for a couple waitresses and cooks in the back. Along the fence sat a large black dumpster.

"Cool," she began removing her gear. The others followed suit. "There's a dumpster right there. We drop this behind there and we get us some food."

"Out of the dumpster?" Cassie asked, pulling her vest over her head.

"What?" Tundra looked at her sister with bewilderment. "No we're going in."

"I don't think we have money for that," Timber added.

"I have it covered, brother, don't worry," Tundra assured him.

With their gear off and in their hands, they slipped out from the shadows.

Crouched over, they clung to the fence till they reached the dumpster. Depositing the gear, they slipped back out and straightened their stance as they stepped into view of the Waffle House.

Cassie pushed the glass door open. A chime rang out. The ladies behind the blue counter with a chrome top turned around in their blue uniforms. One woman stood shorter than the other. Her black hair was long and straight with sunken baggy eyes from years of smoking and late nights. Her counterpart was older with curly blonde hair. Her pink lipstick smile faded at the alarming sight of the dirty, exhausted teens.

"I got this," the blonde said to her co-worker.

Cassie caught a glimpse of the woman's name tag. It read 'Barbara'. She curiously checked the raven haired lady's name tag. The black on silver letters spelt 'Danielle'.

Tundra brushed past her sister and took a seat in one of the blue pleather booths along the glass wall. They followed suit, joining her in the booth.

Timber and Cassie sat across from her and Mac took a seat beside

Tundra.

Barbara arrived with four menus she had retrieved from under the counter. She placed one in front of each of the children. Taking out a pen and her pad, she prepared herself.

"Thank you," Cassie said, taking one of the menus.

"No problem, darling," Barbara replied, she clicked her pen. "Are you four okay?"

"We're fine," Tundra answered, as she flipped opened the menu. "What are you serving?"

"Whatever you like. You all have a beverage in mind?"

They each gave her an order of varying brands of soda. Barbara wrote their choices down and went off to retrieve the drinks. Timber shut his menu and slid it to the middle of the table.

"How are we paying for this?" He asked Tundra.

"Banner's paying," she stated.

"You swiped his wallet too?"

She nodded.

"Damn, what didn't you take from him?" Mac said with a chuckle.

"We shouldn't use up all his cash then," Cassie suggested.

"Pssh," Tundra shook her head. "The man got a Lexus."

"Had a Lexus," Cassie countered.

"Anyway, I'm sure he can afford whatever we take."

"We going for the steaks right?" Mac asked, and put his menu on top of Timber's.

"The only option I see," Timber agreed.

Barbara returned with their drinks on a tray. She distributed them out with a straws. She took her pad and pen back out.

"You ready?" She asked.

"Yes," Tundra answered. "We'll have twelve of the T-bone Steaks."

"Excuse me?" Barbara raised an eyebrow at the mud covered teens.

"Twelve," Mac echoed. "Three apiece."

"Do you have the money to pay for em?"

"Of course," Tundra affirmed.

She produced Banner's wallet from her pocket. She made sure to open the wallet with his credentials facing away from the waitress. Green bills filled the large pocket, and she pulled them out and slapped them on the table.

"That should cover it, Barbara," Tundra gave the woman a cocky stare.

"Okay," Barbara shook her head and took the menus. "Twelve steaks it is."

Barbara walked back to the counter. Danielle met her with a skeptical look. Barbara returned the tray and menus to their stations.

"Did I hear that right?" Danielle asked.

"Yes you did," Barbara walked by her friend to the kitchen.

Danielle followed her. Once out of the eyesight of the kids Barbara stopped. "Something is not right," she said.

"You think?" Danielle concurred.

"You see those kids. They're covered in dirt and they look exhausted."

"What do you think is wrong?" Danielle asked and put her lower lip in her mouth.

"I don't know. Where did they get all that money?"

"What are you going to do?"

"Me?" Barbara scoffed and rolled her eyes at her companion's innate ability to delegate to her. She leaned into the kitchen. "I need twelve steaks dinners!"

"Twelve?" One of the cooks shouted back. "Did a basketball team just roll in here?"

"We're feeding them?" Danielle asked.

"Look, if they did something bad, or they're trying to get away from something bad the least we can do is feed them till the police get here."

"You're calling the police?"

"No, you are."

"Why me?"

Frustrated, Barbara put her hands on her friend's shoulders. "You can do this Danielle, just a phone call. I have to keep up appearances."

"Bullshit," Mac groaned. "Can't we do one thing without the cops getting called on us?"

"Should we leave?" Cassie whispered to her sister.

"You don't have to whisper," Tundra pointed out. "We can hear them, they can't hear us back there."

"We can't leave, I'm starving and tired," Timber said.

"We're not leaving," Tundra answered her sister's question. "They're feeding us, so if anything we get some grub in us. The cops show up, we'll just leave."

Barbara returned to the dining area. She wore a false smile and tried to appear busy with arranging condiments. The kids could hear the steaks hitting the grill in the kitchen. A tempting sizzle in their ears was interrupted by Danielle's voice softly speaking to the police dispatcher.

Time passed while their meals cooked. The smells filled the small restaurant. Their bellies growled in anticipation.

Tundra looked over the condiments and advertisements for dessert left on the table. Mac rested with his head back and mouth open. Timber glared out the window into the night. Soft light reflected off the still wet streets. Cassie noticed he had his collar in his mouth. She spit out her straw and rolled her eyes at her brother's annoying habit.

"Timber, you know mommy hates it when you chew on your collar," she said.

Timber flinched at the mention of her and let the collar fall from his mouth. Mac jolted from his rest and Tundra's eyes shifted to her sister.

Cassie realized her choice of words and felt her face heat up.

"I'm sorry," she said and took Timber's hand in hers.

"It's okay," he replied and gently squeezed her hand. "I still can't believe we are where we are."

"Here we go," Barbara announced.

She carried a large tray over with four steaming dishes. The aroma took over their senses and Barbara couldn't set those plates down any quicker. They tore into their food with silverware and gusto.

Almost done with their first serving Timber noticed the black police cruiser approaching the restaurant. Cassie groaned, she had noticed it too. They all took a look out the window to see the cruiser pulling into the parking lot. Barbara and Danielle noticed it too and gave each other a worried glance.

"Come on," Mac shouted in frustration, as he stuffed his mouth with more steak. "I'm not even near full."

"Keep your voice down," Tundra warned.

Two officers stepped out of the vehicle and made their way into the restaurant.

"So what do we do? Mac asked.

"I'll take care of them," Timber volunteered.

"No," Cassie interjected. "We're not hurting them."

"We're not going to hurt them," Tundra confirmed. "We're just going to move them out of our way."

"How, and can I be a part of that?" Mac asked.

The door opened and the chime rang out. The lead officer, a dark haired gentleman with olive skin, move to the counter. His partner, a pale redhead man with a wide square jaw and curly hair, kept his eyes on the four in the booth.

"Hi ladies," the officer addressed the women behind the counter. "We received a call about four children out past curfew."

"Yes," Barbara answered, as she pointed at the four in the booth.

"They fit the description," the redhead whispered to his partner.

The officer nodded and grabbed the radio clipped to his shoulder. He requested backup and gave the whereabouts of their discovery.

"I need you four to step out of the booth and get your hands up," the redhead demanded.

They stepped out of the booth and raised their hands. Timber gauged the distance between him and the dark haired man. He stood just out of arm's reach, but he knew he could cover the ground before the officer's partner could unholster his gun.

"Don't hurt them," Cassie whispered to Timber.

"I got this," he whispered back.

"I need you four to lay flat on the ground," the dark haired officer ordered.

Timber rushed the officer and delivered a right to the man's chest. Air rushed from the man's mouth. His left hand grabbed the officer by the collar of his bulletproof vest and bounced his head off the counter. Timber watched the red head wrestle with the gun in his holster. The dazed dark haired officer's knees buckled and his body went slack. Timber grabbed the officer's belt and flung him like a bale of hay at his partner. Both officers smashed into the wall and slid to the floor in a heap. Wails of sirens carried in the night air.

"Give this to Detective Banner when he gets here," Tundra said to Barbara. She slammed his wallet onto the counter.

Timber walked over to survey his work. Both officers groaned and stumbled to get back to their feet. Timber gently knocked the dark haired officer back down onto his partner.

"See," Timber pointed at the dazed men. "They'll be fine, besides a headache."

"Whatever," Cassie retorted.

They headed out the door, leaving the employees stunned at what they just witnessed.

"Your steak sucked!" Mac shouted before he shut the door.

"Come on!" Tundra called out to her brother.

They ran to the dumpster and retrieved their gear. Siren wails became louder. Slipping their vests back on and shouldering their arms they jumped the fence.

5:14AM

The sound of toothbrush bristles against teeth mixed with running tap water. Banner and Phillip stood side by side in the station's restroom. Red exhausted eyes stared back at them. Mouth full Banner bent over and spit into the sink. Cupping his hand under the faucet he rinsed his mouth. He cupped both hands and gently splashed warm water on his face.

"You ready?" Phillip asked and dabbed a paper towel against his mouth.

"Yeah," Banner grabbed a towel from the dispenser.

"Been awhile since we pulled an all-nighter," Phillip tucked his shirt in.

Banner threw away the paper towel and headed out of the restroom with Phillip in tow. He grabbed his suit jacket from a desk just outside the door. Slipping it on he retrieved the files he had received an hour ago from Columbus.

"How you think these FBI agents are going to be like?" Phillip asked picking up his jacket.

"I don't know," Banner tucked the files under his arm and moved towards the lobby.

"They better be cooperative," Phillip followed.

"I'm sure you'll put them in their place if they're not."

Banner was already frustrated from being cooped up in his office all night while Jamila's kids were running amok across central Ohio. Phillip's questions, which began flowing unabated twenty minutes ago, dug into his last nerves. He wanted to get on the road and find the kids before harm came to them or anyone else.

They pushed through the door to the lobby. Sarah stood in the center of the lobby speaking to a woman in a dark blue suit. The woman stood tall and slim. Her shoulder length light brown hair matched her caramel complexion. Beside her stood a man with black hair chopped into a crew cut. His wide shoulders and muscular physique gave him the appearance of a former linebacker. The two detectives made their way over to the agents.

"Tommy, Phil," Sarah called out. "These are the agents."

"Special Agent Kwinton Sorento," The six foot five man said.

"Head Detective Thomas Banner."

Banner shook the man's hand. Agent Sorento stood a good three inches over him, and his dinner plate size hand engulfed Banner's. Sorento released his hand and Banner turned his attention to the female agent.

"Special Agent Sidem Balik," she introduced herself, her voice soft but firm.

"See-dem?" He pronounced her name to make sure.

She nodded, her fierce green eyes locked with his. She shook his hand firmly, and quickly moved to introduce herself to Phillip. Introductions aside, Banner revealed the folders in his hand.

"Here's all you need to know on our kids," Banner held the folders up and Sorento took them.

"What about the kidnappers? Do have any suspects? Relatives questioned? Have you had any contact with them?" Sidem asked.

"Winslow didn't tell you?"

"Only information we were given was that four kids were kidnapped and their mother murdered."

"Fucking Winslow," Banner looked over his shoulder at Phillip.

"The man's been locked in his office all night," Phillip explained to the agents. "The officer we lost over the night was a close friend of his."

"I'm sorry to hear that," Sidem said.

"We lost him while chasing after the kids, who were being pursued at the time by mercenaries," Banner informed them.

"Wait, they were being chased by mercenaries? Did they identify themselves as such?"

"Not with their words, but when they had us pinned down with automatic rifle fire and used military tactics to outflank us with ease, it was kinda blatant."

"Not to mention they were not going to be taken alive," Phillip jumped in.

"One car we trapped, they refused to surrender and we had to take them out. The other car they..."

"The kids killed them," Banner finished his partner's sentence.

"What?" Both agents exclaimed.

"I'm still not comfortable saying the kids did it," Phillip said.

"Well, I doubt they snapped each other's necks. We have about ten bodies in the morgue that we cannot find a match to. Whoever these people are their identities are sealed. We're hoping you can help us with that."

"Sure, send the prints to our office. Use my badge number, they'll run it," Sidem pulled a pad and pen out of her pocket and jotted the number down. She handed it to Banner.

"Why these children?" Sorento asked.

"We'll talk all about it in the car," Banner took the paper and gave it to Sarah. He moved past the two agents.

"Where are we headed?"

The agents and Phillip followed the frustrated Banner.

"Columbus," Banner led them out the building. "They assaulted two officers a few hours ago."

"Who? The kids?" Sidem took the lead and led them to a black Ford sedan.

"Yes," the doors clicked and Banner got into the back seat with Phillip. "We suspected they were headed to Columbus when a trucker spotted them running east. That attack confirms it."

"Why would they go to Columbus?" Sorento asked.

"It's in the files."

Phillip adjusted himself in the backseat along with Banner. Comfortable, with his head against the tinted window, he shut his eyes. Banner found himself doing the same.

"Alright," Sidem turned the car on and the engine roared to life. "Kwin, this day just got interesting."

Sorento caught the detectives nestled against the door in his side mirror.

"You two not going to tell us where exactly we're going?" He asked.

Banner opened his eyes.

"Seventy east," he muttered. "Big city, can't miss it. Wake me when you hit two seventy. Read the files. I'll answer any questions you may have. Don't wake me till we get there."

"Let them get their rest," Sidem pulled out of the parking lot.

They traveled down the main street of the small town. She slowed at the debris filled intersection. Caution tape covered most of the street, leaving one lane open for traffic going each way. There were still a couple of wrecked cars with bullet holes in them. An officer, directing traffic, waved them through.

"That explains his story," she whispered to her partner of three years.

"I don't have a good feeling about this," Sorento said after finishing the first page of Banner's report. "Something in there?"

"This guy's thesis is insane."

"How so?"

"Because if he's right, someone made something they will do anything to get back."

She watched a green truck being loaded onto a flatbed. Its windows shot out. She noticed blood on the driver's side door. "That's clear."

7:25AM

Mac sat at the large oak table with his family. His brother and sisters chatted to each other while he watched impatiently. Jamila rose up from the table and collected the kids' plates. She stopped before taking Mac's plate and retreated to the kitchen with full arms.

She didn't even bother to look at him. Slighted, Mac crossed his arms on the table and rested his chin on his forearms. Timber said something funny, he wasn't listening, but the girls howled with laughter. Mac rolled his eyes and stared at his plate.

Jamila returned to the dining room and reclaimed her seat at the head of the table. She reached over and rubbed Timberland's head, who sat next to her. On her other side sat Tundra and Cassie. Mac sat beside Cassie, the furthest away from their mother. Typically he sat beside his brother, but for some reason he was pushed to the edge. She smiled and laughed with her children. He couldn't understand what was so funny. And why hadn't she taken his plate? Did they even know he was here? Even the warmth of home felt absent in this jungle themed dining room.

Mac grabbed his plate and let it fall from his hand. It shattered against the green carpet. The conversations stopped and attention finally locked on him. Jamila stood up her face red and her eyes wide.

Mac could feel the heat arise within her. He stood to meet her. She towered over him like a skyscraper. Her shadow cast him in darkness.

He looked at his hands, stubby little fingers. He looked to Cassie, her baby face stared at him with disappointment. They were toddlers again, and he hated feeling like baby.

"Mackenzie, why did you do that?" Jamila questioned.

"I'm not a baby," Mac stated. "And don't call me Mackenzie. It's a girl's name!"

"Mackenzie, I want you to pick up your mess," Jamila pointed to the mess between them.

He looked to his siblings. "You picked up their plates!"

"Mackenzie, they didn't drop their plates on the floor."

"Stop calling me Mackenzie!"

He picked up his chair and flung it against the wall. The wooden chair shattered to a million pieces. No one budged.

"Use your words, son," Jamila sighed.

She bent down and began picking up the pieces. He looked at his siblings. Their disapproving faces stared back at him. He looked back at his mother. She slid the last piece of chair into place. She took a seat on the repaired chair.

"Come to me baby," her arms stretched out, welcoming.

Mac walked over to her. She scooped him up into her arms and placed him on her lap. The back of his head against her chest, he reveled in the warmth, and her arms wrapped around him.

"Look at them," she motioned to the others.

Mac looked at his brother and sisters. They stared back at the two of them, their faces expressionless.

"You can be the spark that pushes them to greatness or you can be the spark that burns everything around him," she whispered into her son's ear.

He felt her lips on the top of his head. His siblings smiled at them and then turned their attention on each other. They chatted, but he could not hear a word they said.

"Mommy," he said. "I'm scared."

"It only get worse from here," she responded.

The front door shattered into a million pieces. Silenced by the noise, Mac could feel Jamila's arms tighten around him. A hard fabric rubbed against his back and he turned to see a blue vest. He looked up and a blonde man held him.

"Children," the man's low voice called out. "Come here."

7:30AM

Mac eyes opened. A light fog engulfed them in the early morning hour. He sat up, the morning dew soaking his clothes as well as the bushes and tall trees that surrounded them. Timberland sat with his back against a tree, his eyes red. He smiled at his brother then yawned.

"Did you sleep at all?" Mac asked.

Timber nodded and stretched. He grabbed his rifle and moved over to his brother's side. He sat down with him, their shoulders touching.

"Some," he said. "Dreams didn't allow for much though."

"More like nightmares," Mac mumbled.

"We're going to see if we can find a place to shop," Tundra's voice cut in.

Mac turned around to see Tundra and Cassie standing behind him, their guns strapped to their backs. Cassie squeezed some excess water from her shirt.

"So glad I didn't wear a dress today," Cassie commented.

"What you mean by a place to shop?" Mac asked.

"We can't walk around in broad daylight with guns strapped to us,"

Tundra explained. "So we gotta find a place with coats."

"Trench coats to be specific," Cassie added. "Do you think there's a Macy's nearby?"

The two girls walked over to a large tree and began climbing. Both boys remained on the ground watching the young ladies disappear into the thicket of leaves and branches.

"You had a nightmare?" Timber asked his brother.

"It was such a mind fuck," Mac answered.

"Yeah, these past twenty four hours have been insane."

"I wish she was here," Mac yawned and grabbed his rifle. "You think we'll catch these people?"

"Yep."

"How? Columbus is a big ass city compared to our little town."

"Think," Timber watched Mac press a button on the rifle and the magazine clip dropped out. He copied his brother's movement. "We were found playing next to a highway off ramp."

"So that's where the asshole on the phone wants us to go?"

"Well not there specifically, but I feel once we get there we can retrace our steps. We've dreamed about it enough."

"And then what?" Mac pushed the ammo clip back into the rifle. "We kill them and we can stop looking over our shoulders?"

"Doubt it."

"What you mean you doubt it?"

"This feels bigger. Like we're just starting something," Timber slammed his magazine back into his gun.

"Starting what?"

"He's right, you know," Tundra looked up at Cassie.

She estimated they were about fifty feet up. Below them their brothers' conversation carried up to them. With an arm and a leg wrapped around the tree's trunk she kept her other foot on a thin branch. They swayed with the tree as a breeze washed over them. Just above her head, Cassie stood on a branch.

"I wish he wasn't," Cassie said. "I want this to be over with."

Light fog covered the traffic and buildings below them. They had hidden out overnight in a clump of trees next to a busy road. The two girls scanned the horizon for any signs of a store nearby.

"I see a clump of buildings to the east of here," Tundra pointed out.

"Looks like some big ass stores."

"I hope there's a Macy's," Cassie perked up. "I like their coats."

Tundra rolled her eyes and began to climb down.

"I really think Tim Couch can deliver us a playoff victory," Timber stated to his brother.

Both girls landed just a few feet behind their brothers. They brushed leaves and sticks from their clothes.

"We have to go now," Tundra ordered.

Mac and Timber got to their feet. Cassie and Tundra began to remove their guns and armor. The boys followed suit.

"We'll leave this here, grab the coats, come back and head to Alum Creek."

"Where is Alum Creek exactly?" Cassie asked.

"I don't know," Tundra answered. "I guess we can ask when we get to the store."

"Just to be clear," Timber dropped his vest at his feet. "We're stealing these coats right?"

Tundra nodded. "I left Banner's shit at the restaurant."

"Mommy would be so proud of us," Cassie muttered.

"Get it together, Cassie," Tundra countered. "We're stealing from billion dollar corporations. They're not going to miss a few coats."

"And hats," Mac added. "I need a new hat."

"How can you even fit a hat on that big ass afro?"

"There are ways."

"I'm fine with the stealing," Cassie admitted. "As long as we don't hurt anybody."

"Why would we hurt them?" Tundra asked.

"We're not monsters Cassie, geesh," added Timberland.

7:13AM

A uniformed officer lifted the caution tape that bordered the restaurant, to allow Sidem's government issued sedan into the parking lot. A single white news van, with the ABC Six logo on its side, sat against the curb just outside the caution tape. Sidem parked next to an abandoned squad car at the Waffle's House entrance.

"So you think we're dealing with some Frankenstein scenario?" Sorento looked back at Banner as he stepped out of the vehicle.

"You would too if you'd seen what these kids can do," Banner countered.

"Everything you listed is circumstantial," Balik backed her partner. "Besides them catching you off balance, and running fast, you haven't really seen them do anything to support your claim."

The group sauntered up to the entrance. Phillip and Thomas rubbed their eyes to clean the crust from them. Sorento held the door open and they entered the tiny dining area.

"We have bodies in the morgue to back our claim," Phillip pointed out with a yawn.

"But you didn't see them kill anybody," Balik countered.

"Banner," called out a relieved Clifford.

"Cliff, my man how you doing?" Banner met his former partner with a hearty hug and back slap.

"I'm good. Coffee?" Clifford revealed a closed top Styrofoam cup.

"Sure," Banner took the cup.

"I hope I remembered how you take it."

"Three creams and two sugars?" Phillip challenged.

"Three apiece," Clifford corrected

"Lucky guess."

"Pay him no mind," Banner chuckled. "He's a clown."

"Noted," Clifford checked out the two suits behind his friend. "What's with the posse?"

Banner introduced the two agents and his partner. They exchanged greetings and handshakes. Clifford then picked up a folder from the stool beside him. He slapped it on the counter in front of Banner.

"A gift to you my friend," he said.

"The coffee wasn't enough?" Banner flipped open the folder. "What is it?"

"A fire report," Clifford rolled off the tiny steel stool. "I could not get anything on the lost children." The stool screeched in protest and popped up in relief once he was clear. "Or the Agent that took us to the woman's house." He led the group around the counter, past an old man cleaning the condiments station, towards the back.

"So you show up with a fire report?"

"On the night the kids were found, a civilian called in what they believed to be a fire in the woods," Cliff explained.

"You think the kids caused it?" Sidem asked.

The group passed the kitchen. A group of idle cooks yapped amongst themselves. The white walls of the restaurant were stained from years of smoke and burning oils.

"What?" Clifford asked, taken aback by the question. "No, the caller thought they saw a lot of fireworks going off. Figured a storage unit full of the stuff caught fire. They heard pops and explosions.

Anyway, the report says it took a fire truck almost an hour to get to it."

"An hour?" Kwinton asked.

"Yes," Cliff stopped in front of a white door. A silver rectangular sign read 'Manager' in bold black letters just beside his head. "The building was way off of Winchester road, but had no address and no side road leading to it. They finally found a dirt road large enough to fit the truck. They arrived to find the building smoking, but it was no storage unit. The building was massive and it wasn't on fire."

"Shell casings," Banner spoke, staring at a sheet of paper in the folder.

"Thousands of them."

"The Lieutenant described a war zone, but that wasn't the weirdest thing," he fell silent and stared at Banner. Waiting for him to get to it in the report.

"FBI cleared them from the scene."

The officers turned to face the two federal agents. They looked to each other and back at the officers. Sorento shrugged his shoulders.

"Don't look at us," he said. "I was working in the Cleveland offices back then."

"I was a senior in high school," Sidem explained.

Satisfied, Clifford turned the doorknob and entered into the manager's office. The office was rather spacious. Directly opposite of the door was the thin gray haired manager behind his metallic desk. His beard was thick and curly. He stopped his conversation with an officer and Barbara.

The group stepped into the office. To their left, stretched out on a brown leather sofa, lay Danielle. Her raven hair covered her face, and her shoulders rose and fell with every breath.

Barbara turned to see the officers and agents. In her hand she rolled an unlit cigarette between her fingers. She sighed and rose out of her seat.

"Finally," she muttered, making her ways towards the napping Danielle.

"We're sorry for the wait," Sorento stated.

He quickly went through the introductions after Barbara woke her co-worker. Cliff walked over to the manager's desk and spun the monitor around to face them. The others gathered around. Barbara sat on the couch with Danielle. She did not want to see the video again.

"What do you have?" Banner asked.

"We need to interview the witnesses," Sidem said.

"More questions?" Danielle yawned, her soft voice barely registering in anyone's ears.

"Couldn't you get the crib notes from your cop buddies?" Barbara asked, her raspy voice booming.

"Before you do that," Clifford tapped the monitor. "You four need to see this."

He nodded towards the wiry Irish manager. The manager pressed a key and a video began to play. The scene before them showed the kids engulfing their meal when two cops entered the restaurant. Banner noticed the children's grimy appearance.

"What are they covered in?" He asked, his eyes never leaving the monitor.

"Mud," Barbara answered.

"Did they look like they've been hurt? Any cuts or oh!"

Banner couldn't help but exclaim at the quickness Timber displayed. The group gasped as the lead officer was flung across the room. The kids exchanged words amongst themselves, then one of them placed a rectangular object on the counter before leaving. Clifford held the object in front of Banner. He took the wallet and put it in his pocket.

"Why didn't you say they took your wallet?" Phillip asked.

"I knew it would turn up," Banner faced Cliff. "You could've been subtle."

"Had to feed them, didn't you?" Clifford shook his head and gave a hearty chuckle.

"Are they okay?" Sidem asked. The video showed the two waitresses tending to the wounded officers.

"Yeah, just a couple minor concussions and bruises."

"Your file has the tallest of the four kids listed at five six," Sorento stammered bewildered.

"Correct," Phillip said. "How's that for some Frankenstein shit?"

"Can we get to the questions so I can get to bed?" Barbara asked.

7:40AM

"Well if it isn't on the coffee table, then it's either on or under the couch," Charlotte instructed her fiancé, Blake, over the phone.

She leaned with her back against the ABC Six news van. Wrapped in a blue Six News windbreaker over her blood red dress that matched her fiery, dark red hair. She basked in the few rays of sunlight available on this cloudy morning. The warmth felt good against her ivory skin.

"I'm not seeing it," Blake said.

Cast in a moving cloud's shadow she looked up. Gray clouds spotted the sky. Blake began to complain about her inability to keep shit organized. She knew it was time to end this conversation.

"Blake, sweetie, listen, I have to go," she said.

"Alright."

"Make sure Ava actually goes to class this morning," Charlotte rolled her eyes at the thought of her younger sister's insubordination.

"You can't force her to be a journalist," Blake insisted.

"I'm not forcing her and we are not starting this right now," she pushed off the van and headed to its side door.

"Oh yeah, found it! Now I can change the channel," he boasted.

"I can't believe you spent all that time looking for a remote," she shook her head. "Bye."

She flipped her phone closed and stopped at the open side door. Inside, sitting on an upside down green milk crate, was her cameraman Edward Jimenez. He squeezed a blue ABC Six stress ball rapidly in his left hand. His right hand went to work editing the interviews they filmed earlier.

"Why am I editing this here instead of in my comfortable chair back at the office?" he asked.

"We'll go after I speak with the new arrivals. They don't look like they're from Columbus," she stuck her head into the cramped space.

"I didn't think Columbus' people had a distinct look," Edward grumbled.

"That's why you work with the machines and I deal with people. They're way late to the scene and they kept these poor people here waiting for them. I smell feds," she surmised.

"FBI? Don't you believe that's a stretch?" Edward faced her, giving her his undivided attention.

"Not in the slightest and we're going to wait till they exit that building to find out," her eyes gleamed.

"I don't think they want to be on camera."

"They won't, this will all be off the record," Charlotte informed him with a shake of her head.

"Then why bother?"

"Because when I called the sheriff's office that put the APB out on these kids after putting an Amber Alert on them, they didn't mention the FBI being on the case. Besides who pulls a move like that?"

The restaurant doors opened and plain clothed officers stepped out. Charlotte noticed their hurried pace and rushed over. Her red heels clicked loudly against the faded black pavement.

"Hello, I'm Charlotte McCullough of ABC Six News," she cut off a tall, slim woman in blue just before she reached the sedan's door.

With an outstretched hand and a disarming smile she marveled at the woman's dark caramel complexion. She stood several inches taller than Charlotte's miniature five three. The woman hesitated for a moment, taken aback by Charlotte's sudden appearance.

"I would like to know what your involvement with this case is?" She knew she had a short time to get her question in before the typical FBI response. "Are these kids suspects in the murder of their adoptive mother?"

"I'm sorry Ms..."

"McCullough."

"But we have no comments at this time."

The woman opened her car door and waited for Charlotte to allow her by. Charlotte contemplated standing her ground, but thought better and stepped back.

"Ms. McCullough, we are in a hurry."

She jumped at the booming voice behind her. She turned to see a tall black man with a strong build staring at her. She noticed she was in his way, but decided to throw one more question.

"Off the record," she stated. "Why would these kids, after creating the mess they made, come all the way out here to attack a couple of cops?"

Banner sighed and opened the car door. She stepped back to give him room. He put one foot inside of the car and looked back to her.

"They're scared," he said. "They don't know who to trust."

"Is it because there are people chasing them?"

His eyes widened for a moment.

"You're one of those reporters who's been hounding our front desk?" He concluded.

"When four major events happen in a short time and the same group of kids are in the center of it, questions have to be asked."

"Indeed they do," Banner agreed. "Excuse us."

He ducked into the car and slammed the door behind him. Every car pulled out of the parking lot with lights and sirens blaring. Charlotte covered her ears against the noise. She jogged back to the news van, where Edward had an ear bud pressed into his ear.

"What do you got, Eddie?" She asked.

"It's the kids again. They hit a department store now," he removed the ear bud connected to the police scanner.

"Unbelievable, they are not slowing down."

"If you think that's unbelievable you'll love this," a thick, raspy, low voice called out.

She turned around to see the scruffy looking manager standing behind her. In one hand he held a CD case. The other hand removed a cigarette from his lips.

"They don't know I made a copy of this," he held up the CD case for both to see. "But I figured if they're going to cost me money I mine as well make some on the side."

"What's on the DVD?" Charlotte asked, skeptical of the cantankerous man.

"Oh when you see this, you'll understand. This tape defies the laws of nature."

Charlotte knew the man was exaggerating, but knew this could be the piece she needed to blow the story open. Proof that four undersized teens could take out a couple of cops twice their size. This could be the clip played over and over on air.

"It'll cost you though," he added.

"Not paying a penny till I see what's on that DVD."

"No problem," the manager handed over the CD case.

7:45AM

Huddled under a tree, they stared across the parking lot at a Dick's Sporting Goods store. Three cars peppered the expansive parking lot. Through the glass doors they watched a woman set up her register.

"We can't just snatch and dash," Cassie muttered. "We'll need a plan."

"Yeah," Tundra agreed, swatting at an annoying fly. "What you got, Timberland?"

"Umm," he stammered, not expecting to be called upon.

"You read those Tom Clancy's books," Tundra pointed out. "You must've picked something up."

"Seriously?"

"Hey, you don't want me making plans," she pointed to the cars in the parking lot. "I'll end up sending all those cars to the junkyard."

"Fine," Timber scanned the area around them. "We'll have to come up on them from the side. Parking lot is wide open and she'll see us coming. We don't look too inviting."

"See there you go," Tundra gave her brother a supportive pat on the back. "Then what?"

"We rush in fast. Get on the cashier fast, before she can alert anyone, without hurting her," he gave Cassie a smile. "From there we find something to keep her quiet. Tape or something. Move to silence anyone else in the store; then grab what we need and go."

"Sounds doable," Tundra stood up and looked to the others. "You good with that?"

They nodded.

"Follow me," she said.

She led them away from the store before cutting down the parking lot. They stopped in front of a Best Buy adjacent to Dick's and turned right. They moved swiftly in single file towards the glass doors.

"Wait," Tundra whispered.

A beat up, champagne colored Mazda pulled into the parking lot. They huddled together, trying their best to appear as casual as possible.

The Mazda rocked and an obese bearded gentleman appeared from the Mazda. He exhaled from his ordeal then retrieved an empty McDonald's bag from his car. Door shut, he walked to the glass doors.

"I'll take the big dude when he gets through the doors," Tundra whispered to her siblings.

Through their peripherals they watched him approach the store. The glass door mechanics kicked into gear. The doors slid apart and the man stepped into the sporting goods store.

Tundra took off like a cheetah. Swift, long strides brought her to the opening doors. Comforted by the sounds of her brothers and sister behind her she launched herself through the entrance. Her arms wrapped around the employee's neck in a headlock. She swung her legs to one side and landed on her feet.

"Cassie, cashier," she whispered and applied pressure to the man's neck.

Cassie raced past her sister toward the registers. The woman had heard Tundra's sneaker soles slap against the tiled floor. She started to turn to investigate the noise, when Cassie leaped over the register. Her body smashed into the startled woman. With one hand clasped around the cashier's mouth, before she could scream, her other hand stopped them from slamming against the floor.

Tundra felt the hefty man's body go limp and she released him. Nearby she heard a keyboard clicking away. She checked and was relieved to see the man still breathing.

"Mac," she said softly. "You hear the keyboard?"

"I'm on it," he said and moved towards the door labeled 'Store Manager'.

"Do it quietly," she reiterated. "And don't..."

"I won't," Mac confirmed.

Timber stared out at the parking lot. No cars came by and the sidewalks were clear of pedestrians. He noticed a door to his right out of the corner of his eye. He walked to it.

Tundra grabbed the man's hand and dragged his body across the floor.

She stopped once she reached Cassie and the cashier. The woman's eyes were big and her chest rose and fell rapidly.

"Look," Cassie whispered into the woman's ear. "I am going to remove my hand so you can breathe comfortably. Do not yell. I do not want to hurt you."

The ironclad grip Cassie had on the woman's jaw left her no reason to not believe her threat. She nodded with a whimper. Her entire body shook and Cassie removed her hand.

"Is he okay?" Cassie asked Tundra, motioning towards the large mass beside them.

"He's fine," Tundra slapped his belly. "Just put a sleeper hold on him. He went out like a baby."

"Got these," Timber announced, as he dropped three rolls of duct tape between the two girls.

"What are you going to do?" The woman asked, her voice quivering.

"Just keeping you guys quiet," Cassie took a roll of tape and grabbed the woman's hand.

"I won't scream, I promise," the woman sobbed.

Cassie pulled the tape free of the roll and began wrapping it around the woman's wrists. She checked the woman's name tag.

"Then I won't cover your mouth, Keri," she ripped the tape from the roll, satisfied Keri's hands were bound. She went to her legs next. "Still can't have you trying to make a run for it."

"Don't worry, Keri," Tundra added, placing tape over the man's mouth.

"We'll be out of here in a few minutes."

Mac appeared with the manager draped over his shoulder. The manager's long frame forced his hands to drag on the floor behind Mac. He bent over to place the manager down.

"Don't worry Cassie," he said. "I didn't hit him. He actually fainted as I rushed him."

"Then why is there a bruise on his head?" She pointed.

A guilty smile spread across his face. "Keyboard?"

"Cassie, Timber, get the two in the back," Tundra ordered.

"No, no, no, no, don't hurt them," Keri begged.

"Keri, they'll be fine," Cassie held up the roll of tape. "A little duct tape never hurt anyone."

"I don't know about that," Timber chimed in. "You ever try to remove duct tape with a full beard."

"Clearly not," Cassie said, following her brother.

"Not something I want to experience."

Tundra heard a moan and looked over to see the employee she assaulted awake. His eyes darted side to side taking in the whole scene. Tundra patted his belly. The man groaned as he struggled to roll onto his side to see Tundra.

"Sorry I had to come up on you like that," she apologized.

The man growled angrily, his face red and brow wrinkled with rage.

Tundra looked to Keri.

"Tell him to relax. I don't want him having a heart attack."

"Austin, calm down," Keri whimpered, her cheeks wet. "They said they won't be long."

Mac gently tapped his palm against the Manager's face. His name tag read Nathan Waynes. Nathan's eyes opened, revealing confused blue eyes.

"The manager is awake," he said. "Not happy, but he looks fine."

"Good," Tundra crawled over to her brother's side. "You go grab everything we need."

"On it," he said with a smile. He turned to Keri. "Where you keep the clothes and shit?"

Keri motioned behind her, with bound hands, to the back of the store. Mac moved past her and disappeared down an aisle. Tundra looked over Nathan Wayne before turning her attention back to the cashier.

"You have tissue over here?" She asked.

"Behind your head," Keri answered.

Tundra looked and grabbed the box of Kleenex off the register. She tossed the box onto Keri's lap. Keri grabbed a few sheets and dabbed her eyes.

"I'm sorry," Tundra apologized to those bound around her.

"Then why do this?"

"I... we..."

Her mother's image flashed before her. This time there was no smile, just dead eyes, her skin darkened with dried blood. Tundra's jaw shook, her eyes watered. She knew no explanation could justify her action to the captive. She couldn't truly understand all that was happening.

"We have to finish this," her voice cracked and she held out her hand. Keri gave her a sheet of tissue. "They took all we had."

Timber and Cassie stood in the center of a circular rack. Surrounded by women's athletic tank tops, they listened to the male and female workers setting up a shoe display. Cassie studied a white tank top.

"Being albino and all, you really shouldn't wear white. You know, white on white," Timber spoke on a level only Cassie could hear. "You need borders or you'll just look like a blank sheet."

"Don't call me albino, Timber," Cassie left the shirt on its hanger. "Let's get this over with."

Timber nodded and peered through the tops. The two employees had their back to them and the siblings slipped out of the clothes rack. Silently they crept up on the two unsuspecting employees. In unison they struck. A hand over their mouth, they pulled the startled workers to the ground. Each with a roll of tape, they moved quickly. Tape over the mouth in seconds, they bound their hands and feet in rapid succession.

They returned to the registers, the employees draped over their shoulders, to see Tundra wiping her eyes with Kleenex.

"You okay?" Cassie asked.

Tundra nodded. Both placed the employees down gently next to Keri. Keri scooted over to her young female co-worker. She lifted her arms up and brought them down around the crying girl.

"Shh, they're not going to hurt you," she whispered into the young girl's ear. "Can you please take the tape off of her mouth? She won't scream. I promise."

Cassie looked to Tundra who just nodded. Cassie bent down and removed the tape. The girl's sobs filled their ears.

"Keri," she cried out. "What's going on?"

"I don't know, Mary," Keri placed her head on Mary's. "Just try to stay calm."

"Hey guys," Mac's voice entered the gang's ears. "I found the break room and they got vending machines. I'm taking orders."

"Just take all you can," Timber said. He noticed Tundra was overwhelmed. "Stuff em in a bag."

"Excuse me?" Keri asked, unsure who the boy was talking to. She didn't hear anyone.

"He's not talking to us," Cassie pointed out, moving to her sister's side and placed a supporting hand on her shoulder.

"Alright," Mac said. "I'm coming back. I picked up some nice shit."

"Good," Tundra stated.

She moved over to Keri, who was startled by the sudden movement, and grabbed her wrist.

"What are you doing?" Keri asked.

"No!" Mary screamed.

Tundra ripped the duct tape from Keri's wrist and ankles. She did the same for Mary. Tundra pointed over her shoulder.

"Timber get those guys," she said with a sniff.

Timber stepped over her to free the two prone men behind her. Cassie freed the male co-worker beside Mary. Mac's crunching could be heard over the tape ripping as he appeared. Cassie could smell the powdered cheese and looked up.

"Got more of that?" She felt her belly growl in anticipation.

"I heard that," he chuckled and opened a black duffel bag filled with bags of chips, candy bars and drinks.

Cassie grabbed a bag of Doritos and popped it open. Tundra stood up. The tears had finally stopped, but her eyes were red and puffy.

"What's with her?" Mac asked.

"Mac, these past twenty or so hours haven't been the easiest to cope with," Cassie explained.

"If she saw us now," Tundra said, reaching into Cassie's bag of Doritos.

"I just can't believe what we are doing."

"If she was alive we wouldn't be here," Mac countered.

"We don't have time for this," Timber stepped in before the conversation could go any further. "Grab your bags and..." He tilted his head to get a better look at the jackets over Mac's arms.

"We're always running through woods in our dreams," he explained. "I figured these would be better than trench coats."

Tundra took a jacket from Mac. They were hunting jackets with camouflage imprint. She took a duffel bag from him and slipped the jacket on.

"Good job," she said, walking back to the front doors.

"We're just leaving them to alert the police?" Timberland questioned.

"Let them," Tundra called back to her brother.

"Yeah," Mac agreed. "We already got our shopping done. We'll be long gone by the time they get here."

"Alright then, can you guys believe Cassie was thinking of getting a white tank top?" Timber asked.

"What did we tell you about putting white on white?" Mac teased.

"I wasn't going to get it," Cassie defended herself taking a duffel bag and jacket from her brother.

"There's a dark colored shirt in there," Mac added. "Don't want you sticking out like ghosts in the woods."

"Shut up!"

"White on white," Tundra chuckled. "You'll look like a blank page."

"T, not you too."

"Sister, we just helping you out," Timber said. "I'm just glad it's not winter. We'd lose you in a snow drift."

"Ha ha, make fun of the albino girl. That snow shit is going to come in handy one day you just wait and see."

"Mac, you got a sports drink in that bag?" Timber asked.

"Yep," Mac produced a PowerAde bottle and tossed it to his brother.

8:30AM

Banner stepped out of the sedan. He scanned the now crowded parking lot of Dick's Sporting Goods. Tucker took the lead and led them into the taped off building.

The glass doors slid shut behind them. Around them a host of officers and forensic buzzed around the registers. Evidence marked off and camera shutters clicked.

An officer, short in stature with pale skin and light blond hair, approached the group. His jaw clenched and unclenched around a wad of gum. He extended his hand.

"Detective Turner?" He asked.

Turner nodded and shook the man's hand.

"I'm Sergeant Jacob Donners," The Sergeant's breath smelled of sweet spearmint. "First on the scene here."

"Where are our witnesses?"

"They're in the break room in the back," he pointed behind him and past the OSU football display. "Damn mess."

"Anyone hurt?" Balik asked.

"Oh no," Donners shook his head. "Just frightened and sore is all."

"Let's not waste any more time chatting then," Turner suggested.

Donners nodded and led the group to the break room. Officers and paramedics popped in and out of the break room's door like prairie dogs through a dwelling's opening.

Inside the break room the witnesses sat around two circular green tables. A few had blankets draped over their shoulders. They all held opened bottles of water in their hands.

The sound of crushed glass drew their attentions to the vending machines against the back wall. Three of them stood with forensic dusting for prints around them. Two of the machines' doors were laid out on the floor in front of them. The third's door hung loosely on one hinge.

"These kids do not play," Phillip commented and stepped closer to the destruction.

Balik stepped away from the group and towards the witnesses. Banner noticed and followed her. Balik grabbed a seat next to two women, one older than the other. A tall man sat with them, his water bottle shook in his hand. Banner took a seat next to the man. He noticed the Manager title on the man's name tag.

"I'm Special Agent Sidem Balik," she announced to the group.

"Agent ?" The older woman asked. "Are you with the FBI?"

"Are these kids wanted by the Feds?" The manager asked.

"No," Banner answered. "The people after them are."

"There's people after them?" The woman inquired. "That explains what she meant by 'they'"

"What is your name? Did they say anything about their intentions?" Sidem asked.

"Keri, and no, not really," Keri took a sip of water. "The girl, I think they called her Tundra, she said someone took everything from them. Something like that."

"What did the kids take, besides junk food?"

"Duffle bags, jackets," Nathan, the Manager, spoke up. "The jackets were camouflage for hunting. They mentioned the woods."

"Tundra was crying," Mary spoke up.

"Crying?" Banner shifted his attention to Mary. "Was she hurt?"

"Physically they seemed fine," Keri answered. "They moved so fast and were so strong. I think they could've killed us with their bare hands, but the girl, she broke down when I asked her why they were doing this. I couldn't follow their conversation, but it seemed like they lost someone."

"Thank you for your help," Sidem said and stood up.

"Before we leave," Banner looked at Nathan, "did you hand over any tapes of the incident?"

"Yes, an officer has them somewhere around here," Nathan confirmed.

Sidem walked back over to her partner with Banner in tow. The three men were huddled around the vending machines. Phillip guzzled a bottle of PowerAde, a half-eaten Snickers in his other hand.

"What are you doing?" Sidem asked him.

"What?" Phillip asked.

Sidem pointed to the Snickers.

"Right," Phillip took a bite out of the Snickers. "Forensic was done, I haven't had breakfast, and Dick's isn't going to miss this."

Sidem turned to Banner. "Is this how you conduct yourselves in an investigation?"

"What did you get from the victims?" Sorento guided them back on task.

"They just confirmed where we figured they were going," Banner added. "The kids mentioned the woods and stole camouflage jackets to blend into the environment."

"How do these kids even know where to go?" Sorento asked. "You think one of the mercenaries spoke before they died?"

"Logical," Banner shrugged his wide shoulders. "Hard to believe they're going to try and find this place by memory. They were about three when they were found."

"If they are going by memory, this might help us get ahead of them," Sorento pointed out.

The group moved out of the sporting goods store. The parking lot had filled with disgruntled customers and bystanders from neighboring businesses. Amongst the crowd Banner spotted the red haired reporter interviewing a couple of employees in blue tops and khakis.

10:03AM

They stood on the edge of a two lane county road. Traffic was nonexistent as they surveyed their surroundings. Empty fields sprawled behind them. Across the road, towering trees stretched for a mile down the road.

"This feels too familiar," Tundra spoke.

She unwrapped a honey bun from her black duffel bag and took a bite. The others snacked on the last of their food. Black duffel bags hung from their camouflage covered shoulders.

"It's amazing we got this far," Cassie stated, stuffing a square peanut butter cracker into her mouth.

"Come on," Tundra instructed, and stepped onto the empty road.

The soles of their shoes slapped against the asphalt. The cloud cover dispersed and sunlight lightened the dreary day. Tundra spat out a chunk of honey bun.

"Ugh," she groaned. "Honey Buns are only good for a number of bites."

She dropped the remnants on the asphalt and dug in her bag for another treat. Timber stepped over the discarded snack. He shook his head.

"You know you're leaving a trail behind," he called out.

"Timber, that would be true if we were being followed," she countered.

"He told us to meet him here. I'm guessing he's waiting, not following."

"I get that," Timber said, his mouth full of Baby Ruth. "For future reference."

"Noted."

"We're walking into a trap, aren't we?" Mac asked.

"Yep," both Timber and Tundra responded.

They stepped off the road and into the trees. The soft rumble of a silver sedan passed by. The thick forest canopy blocked the sunlight. They stomped through undergrowth, twigs snapping, leaves crunching.

"Shouldn't we, like, not walk into a trap?" Cassie asked.

"Hot fries?" Mac presented his opened bag of Hot Fries to his sister.

She stuffed her hand into the bag.

"That would be ideal," Tundra answered, brushing a tree branch away from her head. "What's our other option? Not like we can boobie trap our own house and tell them to come and try it."

"We could've stayed with the police."

"True, but the folks after us were clearly about to storm the police station. Police can't help us."

"I'm just not comfortable with walking into traps."

They followed one another through the dark woods, stopping every once in a while to survey their surroundings and adjust their course accordingly. They huddled together and stopped at the edge of an open field. Centered in the tall weeds stood a disintegrating building. Its fences were torn down and the sides showed signs of a fire.

"So that's what it looks like," Cassie muttered.

Tundra took a seat at the base of a tree, her back against its trunk. She put her bag in her lap. The zipper clicked rapidly like the snarl of a chainsaw. She pulled out her rifle and swung its strap over her shoulder.

"Ooo," she exclaimed and dipped her hand back into the bag. "Rolo! Thought I smelled Rolo."

Around her, her siblings followed her lead and retrieved their weapons. She held the open Rolo out and they each grabbed one. As they popped them into their mouths, their eyes locked on the shabby building.

"Timber," Tundra called out.

"Five yards separation between us," he said. "Cassie and Mac to the right and left. Tundra, take the front. I got our backs."

"Why not just put our backs together and be a ball of destruction?" Mac asked.

"Because one grenade can wipe out a ball. Spreading out gives at least one of us a chance of survival."

"Don't question the man," Tundra slapped Mac's thigh. "I'll never tease you about playing video games and reading books on and about war all day."

Timber gave a nervous chuckle and scratched his head. He noticed the jacket's collar sticking up and moved his mouth towards it. Cassie's hand shot out and folded the collar down.

"I wasn't going to," he whined.

"Mmmhmm," Cassie smiled and patted his shoulder.

"Anything else?" Tundra asked her brother.

"We should move fast," he glanced over the open field and surrounding trees. "Everything appears clear, but we shouldn't chance it. Fast, like world record breaking fast."

"Alright," Tundra waved her hands. "Move, get in position. Timber, when you say go."

Cassie and Mac moved to get into position. Timber crept up to his sister's side. He placed a hand on her shoulder and squeezed. She rested her cheek on his hand.

"You think we'll survive this?" She whispered.

"I hope we do," he released her shoulder.

"I'm ready," Cassie's voice entered their ears.

"Me too," Mac said.

Tundra looked to Timber. They locked eyes and he smiled.

"I'm behind you. Always," he gave her a shove forward.

Tundra burst from the trees in an eruption of leaves and twigs. Cassie quickly followed with Mac busting free moments later. Timber shot out like cannon fire.

Carrying only their rifles they sprinted across the open field. Their eyes roamed the trees around them, fearful of a deadly flash.

Tundra hopped over a rusted fence and slid to a stop at the wall of the building. The others joined her seconds later. Backs pressed against the building, they collected themselves.

"Everyone okay?" Tundra asked.

They nodded.

"I swallowed my Rolo," Mac muttered and rubbed his throat.

"Ha," Timber teased and pointed to the door further along the building.

"We should get inside."

Tundra shouldered her weapon and led them to the door. She took the handle in her hands and turned it. The door creaked loudly, its hinges rusted, and she held it open just a sliver. Moldy air rushed through the crack. Her face wrinkled with disgust. She tugged at the door, the hinges creaked louder. She pulled harder and the door snapped free of its hinges. She tossed the door aside and stepped into the dark, damp building.

Her left shoulder scraped along the wall with Cassie in step behind her. Decade old buildup of mildew and dirt flaked off her shoulder. She brushed off the cloud of dirt.

Behind Cassie, Mac followed her lead. Timber's hand grabbed his shoulder and pulled him across the hallway. They leaned against the opposite wall. Timber held his hand out as a cloud of dirt washed over the two boys.

"Ew," Mac whined, blowing the dirt away.

"Stop," Timber called out to his sisters. "Me and Mackenzie have to check this room before you pass it."

The girls stopped and looked at their brothers shaking dirt from their afros.

"This place is disgusting," Cassie complained.

"Get to it," Tundra said. "I don't want to be in here for too long."

"Alright," Timber slapped dirt off of Mac's back and pushed him forward.

Mac leaned against the doorway and listened for any signs of life in the room. Besides the sound of tiny scrapes against the decrepit floor nothing alerted him to any threats. He stepped inside. Rifle butt against his shoulder, eyes down the sight, he waved the muzzle around the room and stepped to the right. Timber followed closely behind his brother, his back to him.

"This room is dead," Mac announced. He let the gun hang off his shoulder from its strap.

"What's in there?" Tundra asked quietly from the hallway.

"Looks like a security room," Timber answered.

Mac stood in front of a wall of monitors with their screens shattered. Inside every other monitor were a collection of twigs, dirt and tiny pieces of the walls. A chair, its cushions rotted away, sat in front of the monitors, its metal frame rusted and wheels gone.

Timber tapped an old filing cabinet with his shoe. Squeaks emanated from behind it and four rats ran out over his foot. He instinctively kicked sending an unfortunate rat airborne. Mac ducked as the rat sailed over his head and smacked against the wall.

"What the fuck you throwing rats for?" Mac growled.

"I didn't throw no rat," Timber countered, and pointed at the file cabinet. "It was on my foot."

"Will both of you get out of there so we can move on," Tundra demanded.

They returned to the hallway. Mac ran a hand through his hair, shook off the dirt and mud it had collected.

"There's no rat in your hair," Timber assured him.

"I know."

Tundra rolled her eyes at the two and moved to the next door along the hallway. She followed Mac's example and listened for any danger. Satisfied she stepped inside. She scanned the room with her sister behind her.

A waist high bookshelf stretched around the large room. The shelves were empty, with some of the bookshelf buried under the collapsed ceiling. In the center of the room was a large table snapped in half by the falling debris. The floor dipped where the fallen ceiling separated the table.

Tundra walked past the table. The floor creaked beneath her and water seeped through. Cassie walked to the other end of the room. The floor, once carpeted, was now just thick rancid mud. She stood over a desk covered in weeds, tilted to its right, it drawers scattered around her on the floor.

"Nothing in here to concern us," Tundra called out.

A large crack echoed in the room. Tundra felt the floor move beneath her. She and Cassie locked eyes as Mac and Timber appeared in the doorway.

"What was that?" Mac asked.

"The floor," Tundra whispered, as if the slightest breath would put her in jeopardy.

"Then get out of there," Timber suggested.

"Don't you think I want to do that?" Tundra snapped back.

"Standing here is not going to make us any safer," Cassie pointed out.

"Okay, fine," Tundra leaned forward.

The room shook once more. The old foundation groaned and water flooded her shoes. She froze once more.

"Cassie, you get out of here," her voice cracked.

"Nope," Cassie shook her head. "We're getting out of here together."

"Will both of you just run out of there!" Timber growled.

"When I say go," Tundra said.

"I'm ready," Cassie informed her.

"Go!"

Both girls took off. The brothers stretched their right arms out and took hold of the doorframe with the other. Tundra felt the floor dip to her right. The bookshelf slid towards her and rammed against her thigh.

The muddy floor broke away under Cassie's right foot. She kicked forward with her left. It caught a piece of solid footing, and she launched herself into the air. She soared over a sliding chair.

Tundra kicked through the rotting bookshelf and rushed toward her brothers. She saw Cassie flying ahead of her. Mac's hand caught Cassie's and her momentum knocked them backwards into the hallway.

"Run!" Timber shouted at Tundra.

Tundra screamed and reached for Timber. His hand grasped hers. The floor collapsed and Tundra felt herself fall. Timber tightened his grip and pulled her safely into the hallway.

They crumpled into a heap outside of the caved in room. A rancid cloud covered them. They picked themselves up and moved further down the hallway. Coughing and spitting they stumbled away from the hazardous cloud.

Timber stopped with his back to a door. He shook his head to clear the dust from his hair. The others dusted themselves off.

"This place is hell," Timber grumbled and blew his nose. "No way they can set a trap in this shithole."

He wiped snot from his upper lip and looked to his siblings. They'd grown quiet and something behind him transfixed their gaze. He turned to see the first familiar object in the crumbling building.

A door stood, covered in moss, weakened by years of neglect. The door seemed smaller, less imposing than he remembered. Its light blue color still existed in a few mangy chips of paint that stood defiant against the impending erosion.

The air caught in his chest and his heart clenched in excitement and fear. The others stepped closer to him. A hand, Tundra's, gripped his shoulder. He could feel her anxiety. The small hairs along his body stood on end.

"It's so small," Cassie spoke his sentiments.

"Do we go in?" Tundra asked them, her voice soft and breathless as if all the air left her lungs.

"No," Timber stated.

His hand reached for the doorknob. It was cold and wet. Its rusted edges pricked his hand. He turned the knob and the lock creaked then popped free of the water swollen doorframe.

The door opened to a tiny room. Four beds, two on each wall, pointed towards each other. The mattresses were torn and shapeless. The fabrics were all but gone, and the frames rusted. They stepped into the room.

The door closed behind them.

"This is it," Tundra muttered. "This is what we dreamed about."

"I never thought we would see this place," Cassie said.

Mac walked over to what he remembered as his bed. It was the first bed on the right. He looked down at the small bed. He could see the faded colors of his Teenage Mutant Ninja Turtles sheets. He bent down and grabbed the sheet.

Timber walked over to his bed, across from Mac's. His mattress appeared to have been torn apart by some creature. Possibly a raccoon or possum he surmised. Imprisoned in one of the coil springs was an old friend. He reached through the mess and pulled out a small Batman action figure. He wiped years of build up from its plastic frame and smiled.

"Avoid the noid," Cassie spoke up.

They all looked up to see her holding what was left of her old Noid stuffed doll. She unconsciously tucked him under her arm and continued searching. Her bed was next to Timber's, and near a cabinet. She could hear rummaging inside the cabinet and opened one of its doors. Two rats ran out and disappeared into a hole in the floor. Cassie peered inside.

"More rats?" Tundra stood next to her bed on the far right.

"No," she pulled out a half-eaten yellow box. "Just Operation."

"I remember that game," Tundra chirped up at the sight of the box. "Mac did not like the buzzing noise."

"He was scared," Cassie teased.

"I was scared of no board games," Mac defended himself. "The noise just wasn't natural, that's all."

"This place is freaking me out," Timber declared.

"I barely remember this place," Cassie added.

"Last time we were here," Tundra pointed to her bed, "we were scared out of our minds on my bed."

"That's when we saw that man," Mac said. "The man that keeps taking us away in our dreams."

"Fuck," Cassie groaned. "It really was a suppressed memory."

"What was this place?" Tundra asked.

The click of metal startled them. Their eyes moved to the walls. A metal slab fell from a slit in the ceiling over the door. A series of slabs fell from the makeshift ceiling surrounding the hapless four.

"They built a trap around our room?" Tundra screamed above the noise.

"How is that even possible?" Mac shouted

"What do we do?" Cassie squeezed the stuffed Noid in her hand.

The slabs completed their ring around the group and the four stared at each other with wide eyes. Their hearts pounded so hard they could hear one another's. There was another round of clicks followed by a soft hiss. Cassie felt a soft breeze brush past her white hair.

"Oh no," she stammered. "They're..."

Cassie crumpled to the floor. Tundra rushed to her sister's side, but fell flat before she could take a second step. Mac grabbed the frame of his bed and fought to stand. Timber felt his muscles give out and his will weaken. Mac shook his head stubbornly as his legs slowly buckled.

Overwhelmed, he keeled over. Timber stared at his passed out siblings. He strained to stay up right. He watched the ceiling appear in his vision, then pull away from him till it stopped and his world went to black.

10:32AM

"I am Kwinton Sorento with the FBI," Kwinton called out to the fifty plus officers surrounding him.

They had summoned several officers to a stretch of woodland along Winchester Road. He went on to update to the officers why they were here and what was at stake. Off from the group, his eyes trying to burn a hole through the woodland, stood Banner strapped in a bulletproof vest over his shirt. Phillip and Clifford walked over to join their friend.

"You good to go, Banner?" Clifford asked his former partner.

"I'll be fine," Banner assured him without looking at him.

"If this gets as crazy as you think it will and you can't handle it..."

"I told you I'll be fine," Banner snapped at his former partner.

"What is going on here?" Phillip asked the two men.

"The reason he left Columbus for the small town life," Clifford said.

"What about it?"

"He never told you?"

"There was no reason to," Banner jumped in.

"He should know that I'm the only partner you had that's still alive," Clifford shouted at Banner.

"Whoa, what?" Phillip shook his head at the news. "How many partners have you had?"

"That's not important, Phillip."

"It's five," Clifford answered.

"How does that happen?"

"It's not my fault," Banner snapped.

"He left the city after he nearly got both of us killed," Clifford said.

"Drug bust, turned into a shootout, this guy goes off trying to be a hero. Took three bullets, I took one."

"No one told you to follow me," Banner clarified.

"And no one told you to go into a building full of gang members by your damn self. I'm not leaving my partner in there none of us would. Your first wife left you for that very reason. My wife still hasn't forgiven you."

"You were married before?" Phillip looked at Banner not as the man he once knew.

"Yes, I lived a lifetime before moving out there," Banner finally looked to the other two. "I kept it quiet because I was not planning on being back here. Or going back to that lifestyle."

"I need to know we don't have to worry about you taking off again," Clifford said.

"We've already been in a shootout," Phillip informed him. "He kept it together. We lost an officer, but Banner saved our asses."

"I need you to think of others," Clifford put a hand on Banner's shoulders. They locked eyes. "Don't go chasing medals."

"It was never about the medals, but I've learned we do this together."

"What is going on over here?" Sidem asked.

She too was strapped in a blue vest with large white FBI letters. She had exchanged her flat shoes for sneakers and her handgun was holstered to her side. She added a cap to her ensemble as the clouds cleared away.

"Nothing," Banner answered, walking over to the agent. "Just making sure we're all on the same page."

"And are you? Anything we need to know?"

"We're good," Banner nodded. "Team players here."

"We ready to move?" Phillip asked her.

"Yes, you three will be with my group. We're combing the western half of the woodlands."

10:40AM

Timber sat on his lap. His eyes were glued to the television screen. He squeezed his little hand around the Batman action figure. On the screen, a man dressed similar to the action figure fought off a gang of thugs. Timber bounced with glee at the action sequence.

In the room, seated on the other end of the couch, was Mac and a boy with honey skin and black hair. He was much older than the two boys. They were as entranced with the movie as Timber.

On the floor, giggling loudly, sat three girls. There was Cassie and Tundra seated in a tight circle with another girl who had the same features as the boy on the couch, only her skin tone just slightly lighter than his. The girls held dolls in their hands and were preoccupied with their own world. Their giggles grew louder.

"Ariel, honey," the man holding Timber said. "Please keep it down. You know how much Marvin wanted to see this movie."

"I'm sorry daddy," Ariel said and turned back to shush the younger girls.

"Don't apologize to me," he countered.

Ariel turned to Timberland.

"I'm sorry, Marvin," she said.

"Marvin, Marvin," a voice low in tone echoed in Timber's head.

Timber's head throbbed and the voice calling the faintly familiar name echoed in the depths of his mind. His body felt as if the weight of the world held him down. An oxygen mask covered his mouth and nose. He struggled to open his eyes.

"There you go, son," the voice called to him.

His vision blurry, Timber blinked till the man above him came into focus. A man with thick gray hair and thin gold rimmed glasses stared at him with affection. Timber's eyes widened and the man smiled.

"Twelve years," Porter rubbed his hand against Timber's cheek. "Look at you four. So grown."

Porter stepped back from Timber's bed and looked over to the bed beside him. The kids were lined up side by side in the room. Timber stared at Porter's back.

"Nicolette is up," Porter announced.

Timber noticed the other people in the room moving from bed to bed. He inhaled the oxygen deeply and tried to move. His muscles failed to answer the call.

Porter appeared by his side again and looked him over. He could read a mix of joy and sorrow in the man's eyes.

"I'm sorry," he said to the drugged boy, "for all the dramatics. Once you understand that you are home we will have no need for the sedatives, but right now you are just too powerful. Julie, how are Dorothy and Luther doing?"

"They're conscious and stable, sir," a woman's voice answered.

Porter nodded and moved to the foot of Timber's bed. A woman with dark honey brown skin, several years his junior joined him. She busied herself with an electronic pad in her hands. Timber sensed her unease with the situation.

"Should we lower their dosage?" Julie asked.

"No," Porter answered quickly. "Any lower and we risk losing containment. Look at them, Pam. Strong and healthy. I never thought I would see them again."

Pam finally looked up. She locked eyes with Timber. The panic in the boy's eyes unsettled her and she dropped her gaze back on the electronic pad.

"The helicopter will be here in fifteen minutes, Porter," she said tapping away on the screen. "Maybe you want to try to calm them before we move them."

"Of course," Porter moved back from Timber's bed till he was sure he could be seen by all four. "I know you all have questions and you will know everything soon enough. After losing everything I love twelve years ago there was nothing I'd let stand in my way of getting some of it back.

"For the past decade, we tried to replicate the miracle that gave us you four. But capturing lightning in a bottle twice proved impossible. To manipulate Homo-Sapien DNA and introduce Canis senses is a delicate process, and having our research destroyed all those years ago, made it damn near impossible to replicate. But when our team stumbled across a Dr. Slaughter's ambitious attempt to take credit for my creation we knew we had our second chance.

"Once your blood and tissue samples are analyzed we can finalize the Tamberlane wishes. I can finally be recognized as the man who successfully merged human and animal DNA, creating a human so strong, so elite, there will be no equal to him or her on earth. My name will be remembered forever.

"After my family was killed and my life goals were destroyed. I never thought I'd get this opportunity..."

Timber blinked through teary eyes. Memories once dammed up now flooded his mind. Fantasies of a family searching, hoping, were now drowned in reality.

Porter's words fell on deaf ears. Timber's guilt blocked the nightmare he had awaken to. The only thing present in his world was her. Jamila's hand reached out and touched his forehead. Her fingers ran down his face, stopping to wipe his tears. Her eyes locked with his, a smile on her sweet beautiful face. Her lips moved, but no words reached him. He strained to hear her, but the beeping of machines and Porter's rambling drowned her out.

Timber struggled against the force of the drug to move closer to her. His heart pounded against his rib cage. He wanted to yell, but the sedatives clutched his lungs.

Jamila continued to speak to him. He could read the word 'proud' on her lips. He shook his head, his first real movement. He knew she was not truly here. That some random woman was comforting him, but he felt this was his last moment, to apologize. They had put her through so much and she had always returned it with a smile and love. He needed to express the guilt for every lie they told, no matter how small.

She was their mother, she was their family. No one could tell them any different. She was everything. And more than anything, he wanted to take this chance to tell her goodbye.

"Dr. Porter!" An aide alerted the oblivious Porter.

Porter turned around to see the doctor standing by a struggling Timber. Porter checked the monitor. Timber's heart rate had exceeded one fifty and was climbing. The other monitors showed rising heart rates too, feeding off of Timber's emotions.

"Do we risk increasing the dosages?" Dr. Rachel Stamps asked. She tried to calm the agitated boy.

"No, their systems are going to flush whatever we pump into them now,"

Porter informed. "Get the samples and get out of here."

Stamps left Timber's side.

Timber watched Jamila leave him and fade away. His chest ached and he sat up. He pulled his arms up, the restraints holding him snapped, and he ripped the mask from his face.

"No!" He roared. "Don't you leave me, mommy!"

Porter gave the panic stricken boy one last look and stepped into the hallway. A metal slab slipped down with a loud thud. Around him, the fellow scientists and doctors rushed toward the lobby of the rotting building. Porter pulled Pam close to him.

"How long till the helicopters get here?" He asked.

"Eight minutes," she answered. Her voice rushed. "How did he get up?"

"They're made to produce three times the adrenaline of an average human. It overrode the sedative's effects."

"But that much adrenaline should kill him."

"Not the way I made them."

"Porter, what's the situation?" A heavily armed man asked the scientist.

Porter looked around at the ten mercenaries standing in the hallway.

"Your job is to keep them in there," he looked at the guns in the men's hands. "You do not kill them, you understand?"

"How could they get out? We surrounded them in thick steel," a voice amongst the mercenaries pointed out.

"You do not underestimate them," Porter warned. "We already did so and paid dearly. You cannot fail, and I can't afford to lose them again. The choppers will be here soon. We keep them in there we'll be able to hook up one of the choppers and fly them out in that box."

"Yes sir," the men echoed.

"If they find a way to get out you do not hesitate. You run, or you will pay."

10:53AM

Banner stopped in the cool shadow of the forest. Around him stood twenty or so officers and several dogs. They all stared upwards at the tree canopies.

The thump of propellers against air reached their ears on the forest floor. Sidem reached into her pocket and pulled out her radio. Banner's arm shot upwards and she followed his finger. Through the leaves and limbs she saw the helicopter fly by.

"Sorento," she called into the radio. "I thought we couldn't get a helo out here in time?"

"We couldn't," Sorento confirmed.

Banner took off after the helicopter. Phillip and Clifford cursed and followed.

"Well there's one in the air and it's hugging the tree tops," she informed her partner.

"I hear it, we're coming your way."

"We're in pursuit," Sidem and the others took off after the detective.

10:55AM

Timber stomped his feet against the wet floor, the feeling slowly returning to his limbs. Around him his siblings had risen from their beds.

"I'm going to fucking kill him," Mac growled.

"Not before me," Cassie declared.

She stomped against the floor and the concrete floor gave way. Her shoe pounded against the layer of steel beneath the floor.

"Motherfucker!" The frustrated girl screamed. She punched the concrete, knocking more of it away.

Mac reached over and pulled her out of the small hole she had created.

They peered down at the steel structure beneath them, and then the steel door in front of them.

"They trapped us in a steel cage," Cassie deduced.

"Why don't they just gas us again?" Timberland questioned.

"Probably emptied the tanks the first time around," Tundra guessed.

Timber walked over to his bed and lifted the five hundred pound medical bed. He grunted and let it drop. The floor cracked beneath it. Tundra moved to the steel door and sniffed around its edges. She could smell the men on the other side and hear the clicks of their weaponry. She stepped back.

"Canis DNA," she muttered. "We're fucking lab dogs."

The room shook and debris showered them in dust and mold. Timber had thrown his hospital bed against the wall. He picked it up and aimed it at the steel door.

"It's time we show them what they created," he growled. "Bring the other beds over here. Pile them up. We're busting out of here."

They followed orders and moved to their beds. Tundra rolled her bed in front of Timber's. Cassie brought her bed over and dumped it on top of Timber's. Mac threw his bed on top of Tundra's. They huddled behind Timber's bed.

Timber looked to his siblings. Their eyes were dark black pools, veins and muscles pulsed against the skin, their chests rose and fell quickly. He wiped away excess saliva from his lips.

"When I say go, we drive this fucker through that door and destroy anything in our way," he instructed.

He took hold of the heavy metal frame. They followed suit, each getting a firm grip of the bed and putting their weight behind it. Situated, they nodded confirmation to one another.

"Go!" Timber ordered.

They threw their light weight against the beds. The beds barely budged and they grunted against the weight. The concrete crumbled under their feet from the impact. They pushed and the floor cracked beneath them. The floor gave way and they fell to the steel floor below. Dust showered them and they coughed against the cloud.

"Damnit, now!" Timber shouted.

They grabbed the bed frame and shoved. The metal screeched against the steel and sparks flew. The beds moved and they picked up speed. They slammed into the thick steel door. The door didn't budge and they fell back.

"No," Cassie screamed.

"Don't stop," Tundra shouted.

They climbed back to their feet and pushed against the beds. The door creaked and metal strained. Sweat poured from their pores and their muscles flexed. Metal popped and the door gave an inch.

"Keep pushing," Mac encouraged.

They picked their legs up and drove them back down against the steel floor. Yelling and grunting, they pushed harder. The door groaned and a final pop shook the room. The heavy metal door fell on top of the beds, and the sudden freedom took the kids by surprise as the beds shot forward into the hallway. Screams and gunshots rattled off. The beds caught several mercenaries in its path, driving them across the hallway and through the wall on the other side. In the dusty, poorly lit hallway, they counted only six guards left standing.

They sprang on the startled bunch. Cassie swung hard at a man's chest. His bulletproof vest indented with her fist's impression. She grabbed the collar of his vest with her left and directed a quick right jab to the man's face. His nose shattered, covering his face in blood. His knees buckled and Cassie wrapped her left hand around the man's throat.

A second man stepped up to her, his gun pointed at her chest. She swung with her left guiding the bloody man's head across his partner's head. The man's skull fractured against his partner's face. Cassie released the man and both fell at her feet. Tundra released the man in her grip and his lifeless body fell.

They turned around to see Timber retrieve a gun from a man whose face he had smashed in. He checked the clip of the rifle then looked at Mac. Mac held a gun and began creeping down the hallway toward the lobby.

"There's more this way," he called back over his shoulder.

Timber followed and both girls grabbed a rifle from their victims. Mac stopped at the edge of the hallway. He could already smell the men awaiting them in the lobby.

"There's five out there," he told Timber.

"We'll step out and take them out, then find Porter."

"Think we should get in a shootout with these guys?" Tundra asked.

"Our reflexes should be faster than theirs, and we can see in this poor lighting. We move fast we should get them before they fire a single shot."

"Do you hear that?" Cassie asked.

They settled down and took in all the sound around them. The nervous breathing of the men in the lobby. The chirps of birds and the sharp sound of blades slicing through air.

"A chopper?" Mac questioned.

"They're on the roof!"

Timber shouldered his weapon and shot out from behind the hallway. A trained killer aimed his gun on the sudden movement. Timber squeezed the trigger and the killer's body jerked back. A spray of blood painted the wall behind him.

11:05 AM

"We found the building," Sidem shouted into the radio.

She rushed across the open field with her search party all around. Far ahead of the group were Banner and Phillip. Clifford had fallen back and was now behind the entire search party.

Above the building hung two helicopters, one on the roof and another hovering nearby. Inside the rotting building the familiar pop of gunshots reached her.

"We have gunshots. Get the medics up here."

Banner stopped at the wall to catch his breath. Phillip leaned beside him sucking in gulps of air. An open doorway stood just a few feet away, its rusted door lying on the ground.

"We have to wait for backup, Banner," Phillip pointed out.

Banner nodded and checked his pistol. He knew his partner was right, but he didn't want those people on the roof to get away. Not while he could do something about it. Another burst of gunfire rang out.

"We have to go," Banner shouted to his partner. "They need us."

He rushed through the doorway into dark dank building. He turned on his flashlight. His nose hairs curled at the acrid smell. He shook his head and pushed forward.

"What the fuck is that smell?" Phillip whined behind him.

"Shut it," Banner warned.

They walked further down the hallway. Past the cave-in, they stopped when they found six bodies strewn along the dirty floor. He pulled out the radio from his pocket. "Sidem, we have six bodies in here." He looked over at the large hole in the wall. Shining a light inside, he saw medical beds. "Maybe more."

"Banner, you fucking stay where you are," Sidem ordered.

"Can't, I hear someone," he said.

Banner moved forward towards the lobby. He stepped into the lobby and a shot zipped past his head. He dropped to the ground.

"Phillip!" He called out.

"I'm fine, goddamnit," Phillip clung to the floor. "Clifford was right, you're going to get me killed."

"Naw, your reflexes are sharp," he slapped his partner's shoulder.

"Police! Put your gun down!"

"They fucking shot me," the wounded man called back.

"We can get you help, just put the gun down."

"I don't want your help."

"Where are they?"

"Up."

A shot echoed from a different angle. Banner turned his head in time to see Tundra disappear around the corner. Banner moved to get on his feet.

Phillip grabbed him. "What are you doing?" He asked Banner.

"Tundra shot him, we're clear to move," Banner pointed to the far end of the lobby.

"Tundra did what?"

11:09AM

"Fucking Banner is going to get himself killed," Tundra told Cassie.

"He's here?" Cassie asked.

Cassie stepped onto a rickety metallic stairway behind Mac. Timber led them upwards to the roof. Tundra fell in line behind her sister. She looked back to the corner. Banner hadn't arrived yet, but she could hear him stomping through the dark.

Their feet echoed against the metal. Above them the thump of propellers against the wind drowned out the anxious and frightened yells of the fleeing scientists. Timber could tell one set of blades had lifted off the roof. He growled and leapt over the few remaining stairs and landed on the roof.

One black helicopter had cleared the roof and was making its escape. Its twin hovered several feet above the roof and began to pull away from the building. Timber caught sight of Porter seated between an armed guard and his assistant Pam.

He raced across the roof. The aircraft cleared the building by over ten feet both horizontally and vertically, but Timber was determined to reach him. He launched himself off the edge of the building. Wind rushed past his ear softening the roar of the engine. The craft grew closer and he landed on the skid.

The helicopter jerked and tilted against the added weight. Pam and the others in the cabin screamed. Timber clutched the doorway with one hand and grabbed the stunned guard by his vest. Porter grabbed the man's shoulder with one hand. Timber ripped the guard from Porter and flung him out of the cabin. The engines drowned out his screams.

Timber reached for Porter. Porter buried the guard's pistol into Timber's shoulder and pulled the trigger. Timber roared, the pain sudden and overwhelming. Blood spurted from his back. He lost his grip and slipped.

Porter hooked his arm under Timber's and held the boy against him. Timber's blood soaked his lab coat. He pressed his lips against Timber's ear.

"I'm sorry, but you have to control your heart rate or you'll bleed out," he warned.

Porter turned his attention to the men in the pilot's seats. His headset connected him to them. "I need you to take this chopper back over the building," he instructed the two helmeted men.

"No can do sir," the pilot responded. "This place is crawling with cops. My job is to get you out of here."

"You take us back now," Porter shouted. "He will die before we can get him adequate care."

"Sir, isn't the point is to get them anyway we can?"

"No," Porter screamed, his voice high and his eyes wide. "Not anymore. I cannot have them die on me. I will not kill my son."

"My instructions were clear. I..."

Porter pointed his gun at the co-pilot.

"Holy shit, man," the co-pilot exclaimed. "What the fuck are you doing?"

"I will put a bullet in your fucking head if you do not take us back," Porter looked at the red pool spreading down his coat. "We are wasting time! They will have medical care down there!"

The pilot looked to his co-pilot with a smug look. The co-pilot returned the look with concern in his eyes.

"He won't shoot," the pilot said.

Porter took the gun and pressed it against Pam's head. He pulled the trigger before the woman could react. Everyone in the cabin screamed. Pam's body slumped over in the seat. Her blood covered those seated beside her.

"I've been fucking that bitch for years," Porter stated. "I will not hesitate to put a bullet in your co-pilot's head."

"Dammit, Dominic," the co-pilot stammered. "Fucking do as he says."

"I..."

"Three seconds and we all go our graves," Porter warned.

Dominic swung the helicopter around. Porter pulled Timber closer to him and placed his cheek against the boy's. Timber could feel the man's tears against him.

"I'm so sorry, Marvin," he whimpered. "Deep breaths. You're bleeding too much."

Porter looked over Timber's shoulder. Below them, huddled together, were the other three. Standing with them was a large black man with a police windbreaker on. He loosened his grip on Timber as Dominic lowered the aircraft.

"My name is Timber," Timber remarked weakly.

Porter released Timber. He fell into the arms of his siblings. The helicopter peeled away from the building.

"Oh my God, Timber," Cassie exclaimed. Her brother's blood on her hands sent her into a panic.

"We have to stop the bleeding," Tundra shouted putting a hand over the gunshot wound.

Mac ripped his shirt and quickly tied it around his brother's bleeding shoulder. Timber's limbs shook violently. He sucked in deep breaths of air and shut his eyes.

Sidem stepped onto the roof. The black helicopter disappeared over the tree line. She rushed over to the huddled chaos. Banner had propped Timber's head on his lap and was applying pressure along with Tundra.

"We need EMTs up here now," Sidem barked into the radio.

September 22nd, 2002

12:48PM

Banner, with a duffel bag over his shoulder and a brown paper bag in his hand, stepped out of the Children's Hospital elevator. The hallway was white, painted with flowers and cartoon characters. He passed several nurses and doctors along his way to the kids' room.

"Detective!" A vaguely familiar voice called out to him.

Banner looked over his shoulder to see the red haired reporter make her way to him. Charlotte McCullough stopped running towards the stunned man once she had his attention. She stuck her hand out with a smile. His massive dark hand covered her petite hand.

"I almost didn't recognize you in your street clothes," she said commenting on his jeans and hoodie.

"Well, I am off duty, Ms. McCullough," he pointed out. "What are you doing here?"

"My fiancé is an intern here," the reporter clarified. "We have lunch together whenever we can."

"Oh, okay."

"But don't think I didn't notice that the kids who went on a rampage have been admitted here."

"Only one have been admitted."

Banner began to walk away from the reporter. She followed.

"I know," she said. "Timberland Dunne was shot, correct? How is he?"

"Did your boyfriend tell you that?"

"Fiancé," she shook her head, "and no he didn't. He works for a different ward, and besides, I wouldn't put him in that position."

They turned a corner and passed the nurses' station. The lower half of the walls were painted to resemble a meadow full of sunflowers. Down the hall was an officer seated beside a door.

"It's good to know you have boundaries," Banner commented.

"I'm not a bad guy, Detective Banner," Charlotte defended herself. "I'm just curious to know why and how four kids were able to cause so much damage in such little time."

"I am as curious as you are."

Banner stopped beside the uniformed officer. The officer grabbed a clipboard with a list of names on it. Charlotte crossed her arms. "Why are highly skilled mercenaries chasing these poor kids? And how are they still alive?"

"Who told you about the mercenaries?" Banner demanded, frustrated at the leak.

"I'm good at my job, Banner," Charlotte smirked.

"Banner," the officer stated. "You are on the list."

The officer unlocked the door to hospital room five-two-six. The chatter of teenagers reached their ears. The officer turned back to face the two.

"Who is she?" He asked.

"Someone who is not allowed in the room," Banner answered. "Make sure she does not talk to these kids."

The officer nodded. Banner entered the room and shut the door. He heard the officer lock the door behind him.

Seated on the bed were Timber and his siblings. Timber was cloaked in a white gown, his left arm in a blue sling. On his face he wore a wide smile, while Tundra spoke enthusiastically to him. The sisters and his brother were dressed in scrubs.

"Tommy Banner, my man, Charlotte bugging you too?" Mac called out to the detective. "Grab a chair, get over here."

"She talk to you?" Banner asked.

"Nope, just hear her yapping to every new cop they put out there."

Banner walked to a table with chairs around it. He grabbed one and noticed another chair in pieces under the table. He carried the chair over to the bed and sat down. The chatter faded away every pair of eyes were on him. "Who broke the chair?" He asked.

"Who you think?" Tundra motioned her head at Mac.

Mac shrugged. "They tried to separate us," he explained. "I had to let them know we wasn't having that."

"How are you, Timber?" He asked with a sympathetic pat on the boy's good arm.

"I'm good," the boy answered. "Clean hole in my shoulder blade, and the pain killers work like a charm."

"The bag, Tommy," Mac pointed.

Thomas Banner could read the eagerness on their young faces. He lifted the brown paper bag and placed it on the bed. Mac scooped the bag up and opened it.

"The mortician was able to get her jewelry cleaned," he explained.

Mac pulled out Jamila's necklace. He felt his throat tighten and handed the necklace to Tundra at the foot end of the bed. Tundra stared at the silver necklace. The afternoon sun reflected off its freshly polished surface. Mac pulled out his mother's watch. Cassie's arm immediately stretched out for it. Mac handed it to her. Tears rolled down her cheeks.

"What else is in there?" Timber asked his brother.

Mac retrieved the largest and last item in the bag, a rectangular silver wallet. The wallet was clasped shut and Mac released the lock.

"That was in her purse," Banner explained. "Most the stuff in her purse was work related, but I felt you would want this."

Inside the wallet were four pockets. One was filled with bills and loose change. Another pocket held her credit cards. The last two pockets were filled with wallet sized photos of her with her kids. Mac pulled out a photo of the two of them together. He was young in the picture. He dropped the wallet on Timber's lap and stared at his younger self. Timber took the wallet and retrieved a photo himself.

"Thank you for this," Tundra clasped her mother's necklace around her neck.

"No problem," Banner patted the duffel bag on his lap. "Also got your clothes from your home."

"I hope you didn't grab my Hanson shirt," Cassie sniffed. She studied her mom's watch around her wrist. "I would like for that moment to be forgotten."

"Didn't see it."

Banner watched them pass photos around and share smiles. Tears began to subside, their emotions subdued.

"You're holding out, Banner," Tundra stated.

Banner reached into his pocket. He pulled out a set of keys. The metal jingled like wind chimes.

"I was still deciding on rather or not to give you four these."

Tundra held her hand out and he handed the keys over. She looked the keys over.

"Your home is sealed," Banner informed.

"And the storage unit?" Tundra asked, holding the key to it between her fingers.

"Has not been looked at yet. It's actually here in this city. You wouldn't happen to know what's inside of it?"

"Never knew of it till now."

"Thought so."

"You'll let us check it out first?"

"Are you going to give the keys back?"

"No."

"Timber," Banner said. They turned their attention to him. "Once

224

you are well enough to be released you four will be put into protective custody. We aren't sure when, but you will be taken to court to see what charges will be brought against you."

"Banner, you can stop right there," Tundra cut him off. "We are not going anywhere with you or anyone else."

"Tundra, we will have to protect you."

"By putting us in jail?"

"We don't know if that will happen."

"Tamberlane," Cassie interrupted the two.

"What?" Banner asked.

"The man who took us, Nathaniel Porter. He mentioned something about the Tamberlane family financing his research."

"Did you find anything on him?" Timber asked.

"Nathaniel? We're still looking, but there are a lot of matches to that name and none are scientists so far. We'll check out this Tamberlane family."

"This is why we can't go with you," Tundra groaned. "You're too slow and before you find these people they'll find us."

"And you think you'll be able to find them faster?"

"No, I don't know what we're capable of," Tundra hopped off the bed. "They created us in a fucking lab. We put anyone between us and them, and they will just kill them like they did our mother."

"I understand you are afraid, but you can't let that lead you to irrational decisions."

"Don't call her decisions irrational," Mac interjected. "She's right. They'll kill anyone and destroy anything to get to us. He said so. We have to keep as few innocent people between us and them. You find us the Tamberlane family, Nathaniel Porter, or both, and we will kill them before they kill anyone else."

"Listen to yourselves," Banner countered. "I'm still trying to wrap my mind around this whole genetics stuff."

"Get on the ball, Banner," Timber shouted. "You either help us or get out of our way."

"I can't let you do this," he pleaded.

"You have no choice," Cassie explained. "You can't stop us. No one can."

ABOUT THE AUTHOR

Marcus Broome was born in Charleston, South Carolina and resides in Columbus, Ohio. He is currently writing the next installment in the series.

www.ingramcontent.com/pod-product-compliance
Lightning Source LLC
Chambersburg PA
CBHW070746180626
46818CB00007B/3009